ATHLETES AND ALIBIS

DUNE HOUSE COZY MYSTERY

CINDY BELL

ISBN: 9781723789755

❀ Created with Vellum

CHAPTER 1

"*P*ilot! Get back here!" Suzie laughed as she watched the dog spray sand up from beneath his paws. He ran towards Jason so fast that she wondered if he might take off and fly. The sunny morning made the outstretched ocean sparkle, as if it too was quite excited by the event that was about to take place. The *Seaside Relay Triathlon* had chosen Garber as the location for their race this year, and Suzie couldn't be more thrilled. *Dune House*, the bed and breakfast that she and her best friend, Mary ran together in the small beach-side town, was packed to the gills. She'd managed to sneak out for just a little while to give Pilot a chance to run, as most of the guests were participating in early morning activities. They were all training before the big race.

"Hi buddy!" Jason laughed as the dog jumped up to greet him. Pilot was well-behaved with the guests, never jumping up or barking at them, but Jason was his friend, his buddy, who loved to play with him. "Hi Suzie, what a beautiful morning, huh?" He looked at her, his eyes sparkling just like the sea.

"Gorgeous." Suzie took a deep breath of the salty air and closed her eyes as a feeling of content-ment rushed through her. "Are you excited about the big race?" She offered a warm smile. There was no doubt that he was, he'd been talking about it for weeks. Jason, in his thirties, was fit and spent much of his free time, when he wasn't wearing a badge and keeping Garber safe, engaged in physical activi-ties. He and his wife, Summer often ran together on the beach. Suzie would wave to them from the wraparound porch of *Dune House*. She could recall having that boundless energy, but since she'd hit her fifties she didn't feel it so much. She could be moti-vated to go for a leisurely swim, or even chase Pilot around for a little bit, but most of the time she preferred to cheer athletes on rather than join them.

"I think so, I hope so. I've been going over the

security plan all morning. I've been able to borrow some officers from Parish to help." Jason grinned as he ran his fingers through Pilot's golden fur. "I'm really excited to see the Parish team compete. There is some pretty stiff competition though. I still can't believe they chose Garber to host the race."

"I can see why they did. It's a beautiful place, and one of the safest, thanks to you." Suzie smiled at him. "I'm confident that you've made all of the arrangements and the race will go off without a hitch."

"Aw, that's kind." Jason winked at her as he tossed a shell towards the water for Pilot to hunt down. The yellow Labrador leaped into action, as if he was trying to prove that he was every bit the athlete that Jason was. "Honestly, I'm pretty excited. Just to get to witness some of the best local athletes in action is an honor."

"They're coming in from all over the state, right?" Suzie held in a laugh as Pilot pounced on a wave that rolled towards the shore. It must have stolen his shell.

"Some are, but most are from nearby cities. Stuart Pike will be here, can you believe that?" Jason shook his head, then blew some air through his lips. "That's pretty amazing."

"Stuart Pike?" Suzie raised an eyebrow. "Should I know him?"

"Oh, maybe not. He's pretty well-known in the race community. He's one of the top swimmers in the country. I was surprised that he decided to participate in this competition, as he's already won it three times. I thought he was taking this year off to have a break and give some of the younger athletes a chance." Jason took a step back and laughed as Pilot shook off his wet fur.

"Wow, that should really put a spotlight on the race." Suzie smiled at the thought. It wasn't that long ago that she was more in touch with the happenings in the fast-paced news and entertainment world. As an investigative journalist, stories she worked on had led her down some interesting paths. But none had been as rewarding as the path that led to *Dune House*.

"Yes, it should. Thanks for the chat, Suzie, I'd better finish up my run." He gave her a short wave, then took off across the sand. Pilot ran after him for a few minutes, then slowed down, turned, and bounded back to Suzie.

"Ready to go back, huh?" She grinned as she crouched down to pet him. "All right, boy, let's get you some water."

As they started back towards *Dune House* she noticed two men make their way onto the beach from behind one of the local restaurants. Their brightly colored swimwear drew her attention first, but their unfamiliar faces left her curious.

"Suzie!" Mary's voice rose just above the sound of the waves.

"Hey there." Suzie smiled as she turned to face her friend. "You were able to get away?"

"Yes, everyone is out of the house, and lunch is already prepped. I thought I'd join you for a few minutes. It's so gorgeous out today." Mary gave Suzie a quick hug.

"Yes, it is. You just missed Jason. He's pretty excited about the race." Suzie glanced back at the two men and found that they were headed in their direction. Pilot spotted them, too, and began to run towards them. He bounced and darted back and forth, not getting too close, but tempting them to play with him.

"Aren't you a beautiful pup?" The taller of the two men smiled at Pilot.

"He's friendly." Suzie smiled as she walked the short distance between them, with Mary at her side.

"I can see that." The taller man nodded, then

held out his hand to Pilot. Instantly, the dog nuzzled it.

"He's yours?" The shorter man inquired.

"Ours." Suzie tipped her head towards Mary. "I'm Suzie, and this is my friend Mary."

"Simon." The shorter man smiled at Suzie then Mary. "It's nice to meet you."

"You as well." Mary returned the smile. "Are you here for the race?"

"Oh yes." Simon laughed. "We sure are. This is Stuart." Simon smiled as he gestured to the man beside him. "You might have heard of him, or seen him practically naked plastered all over the place."

"I wasn't naked!" Stuart laughed, and his cheeks grew pink.

"I'm not sure I have?" Mary glanced from him, to Simon, then to Suzie.

"Stuart Pike, he won the competition last year —" Suzie began to explain before Simon interrupted.

"And the year before, and the year before that." Simon laughed and clapped his friend on the back. "He's the golden boy."

"You know it's called a relay." Stuart raised an eyebrow as he looked over at Simon. "If it weren't for all of the hard work that you and

Annabella put in, we would never get to that trophy."

"Sure, sure." Simon rolled his eyes and crossed his slender arms across his stomach. "He's always pretending to be modest. But we all know that if he didn't swim so fast, our team would never win."

"Well, we're glad to have you here, Stuart." Mary smiled at him.

"That's so kind of you, Mary." He looked into her eyes for a few moments. "If you'd like an autograph, I can arrange that."

"Ouch, there went that modesty." Simon laughed and nudged his friend with his elbow.

"I'm just trying to be polite." Stuart grimaced.

"Good thing your mom is in town. Maybe she can knock that ego of yours down a few notches." Simon grinned.

"What?" Stuart's tone grew sharper. "What are you talking about?"

"Oh, I thought you knew." Simon took a slight step back. "Never mind, we can talk about it later."

"Or now." Stuart's jaw clenched.

"Relax Stuart, she told me she was placing a bet on you." He grinned. "I told her that was going to be a good bet."

"You spoke to her?" Stuart's tone grew harsher.

"We run *Dune House* and we'd love to have an autographed picture to put up on the wall there." Suzie offered in an attempt to ease the tension between them.

"Great. I'll make sure I get one to you." Stuart turned his attention back to her, his expression friendly once more.

"I'm so excited for the big race. I'm sure you'll do just fine, but you'd better watch out for the team from Parish, they're going to give you a run for your money!"

"I'm sure. I know all about the team from Parish." Stuart's expression darkened just slightly. "Well ladies, I need to train a bit more, but it was nice to meet you."

As he jogged off across the beach, Simon chased after him.

"Ouch, Suzie." Mary laughed as soon as the two men were out of earshot.

"What?" Suzie's eyes widened with innocence. "Nothing wrong with a little friendly feuding. We have to support our local athletes, right?"

"Sure, but did you see his face when you mentioned the team? I guess he doesn't like competition." Mary grinned.

"You might be right about that."

Suzie stared off in Stuart's direction for a moment, then followed Pilot and Mary back towards *Dune House*.

When they arrived at *Dune House*, they were greeted by a tall, slender woman with long, golden hair, made even more golden by the strong sun.

"Hello there." She smiled as she offered her hand to each of them. "I hope you don't mind me stopping by. I'm Alana Deleon, I own the company that organizes the race. I just wanted to check in with each of the places where athletes are staying. We hold our athletes to very high standards, so if you have any trouble with anyone, please don't hesitate to inform me."

"It's nice to meet you." Suzie shook her hand, then smiled. "I'm Suzie, and this is Mary. So far, we've had no trouble, and I'm sure everything will go smoothly."

"Wonderful." She pulled her hand back from Mary's, glanced over the water, then back at them. "I have to say, we couldn't have picked a more beautiful place for the race."

As she walked away, a sense of pride swelled in Suzie's chest. Alana most likely saw many beautiful places in her travels, but it was clear in the way she spoke about Garber, that this really was one of the most beautiful she'd seen.

Mary brushed the sand from her feet, then stood up from the bench on the porch. The warm sun beat down on her neck and shoulders, despite the long auburn and gray hair that hung there.

"It was nice of her to stop by." She squinted up at the sun for a moment. "It's going to be pretty hot today."

"Seems like it. Hotter than they predicted." Suzie finished brushing the sand out of Pilot's fur, then let him loose to head into the house. "We should make sure we get some extra cases of water from the store. I'm sure our guests will go through them pretty fast."

"I'll put it on the list." Mary nodded, then followed her into the house. Despite the rush of guests that checked in the day before, *Dune House* was in good shape. Between her and Suzie they managed to keep things tidy and running smoothly. Most of the time.

"So, exactly how many athletes do we have staying here?" Suzie grabbed a broom and began to sweep the hallway.

"Well, the team from Parish, along with their coach. Michael, Shelly, and Andrew. Their coach is

Jen. She said it was just easier to have everyone here than to have to drive back and forth for all of the training and events."

"Oh right, Jen. I met her yesterday. She seems very determined." Suzie flashed her a smile."

"Yes, determined is one way to put it." Mary laughed as she washed her hands. "There is also a team from out of state, Sam, Ali, and Carter. Their coach is staying somewhere else, though."

"Wow, it was such a rush yesterday to get everyone checked in that I didn't realize we had so many talents under one roof." Suzie scooped up the sand she'd swept up, then tossed it in the garbage pail in the kitchen. "We'd better make sure there are lots of extra towels available. I imagine as much as they're working out they're going to need them."

"Good idea, I'll check on that." Mary started towards the stairs that led to the linen closet, then paused at the bottom. "Oh, don't forget Charles is staying here, too. He's one of the officials that will judge the race. In fact, he requested a wake-up call at seven tomorrow morning, and I'm not sure that I added that to the log and his file."

"I'll check on it." Suzie headed for the front desk. As she skimmed over the files for each of the guests, she noticed that Charles had quite a few

11

requests. Lemon water first thing in the morning, along with a few other dietary needs. From the sound of it, she would guess that he was an athlete, too. As she recalled from the night before, he was quite fit. Perhaps he had once participated in the race himself. After she added the request for a wake-up call, she started back towards the kitchen to get the table set for lunch. A light knock on the door, followed by it swinging open, turned her attention towards it. Jason stepped inside, his face red, and his collar soaked with sweat.

"Hey Suzie, any chance I can get a bottle of water? I forgot mine this morning."

"Of course you can, come sit." She grabbed a bottle of water from the fridge. As he sat down at the long, wooden dining room table she handed it to him. "You look like you pushed it a little too hard out there."

"It was a bit hotter than I expected." He nodded and cracked open the bottle. "Might have to go for a swim to cool off."

"Good idea." Mary stepped off the stairs that led into the kitchen, then joined them in the dining room. "It's certainly toasty enough."

"I have a feeling everyone is going to have that same idea." Suzie sat down at the table and gestured for Mary to join them. "What else do you have planned for today, Jason?"

"I'm going to go over the race zones, make sure there are no security flaws. Then I've promised to walk Alana, the organizer of the race, through a few of our emergency plans. She seems a bit nervous. Then of course there's the dinner at the diner tonight." He met Suzie's eyes. "You two should come to it, the diner is hosting it for all of the athletes and staff of the race, and security was invited." He grinned.

"But we have so many guests and—"

"And most of them will be at the dinner." Mary patted her shoulder. "I can handle whoever stays behind. You should be there, Suzie. Jason would like your company, I'm sure. Right, Jason?"

"Right. I'm sure it'll be a nice time. You should bring Paul." Jason finished his bottle of water. "Thanks for this."

"All right, I'll see if he'd like to do that. It's been so busy we haven't had much time together since he came in from his last fishing trip. I'll get you another bottle." She walked back towards the kitchen and grabbed him one.

"Thanks Suzie." He met her halfway and took it from her.

"See you tonight."

"See you then. Bye Mary!" He waved to them both as he headed out through the side door in the dining room.

"Are you sure you don't mind, Mary?" Suzie looked over at her with some concern. "I hate to leave you alone when we have guests."

"I need to work on the linen closet, anyway, it was a bit of a mess, I guess guests have been helping themselves. Besides, most of them will be at the diner, and I can always invite Wes to join me. He can be quite helpful when he wants to be, you know." She smiled fondly at the thought of him. "If no one shows up for dinner, then we can just enjoy it ourselves."

"That does sound nice." Suzie smiled at the thought of the two of them together. "If we head out now I bet we'll be able to catch the cyclists when they come through the park."

"Oh, that sounds great. I saw a few of the runners practicing earlier today. I wish I could be athletic like that!" She sighed and patted one knee. "Maybe one day."

"I'm sure you will." Suzie smiled. "It was a nice idea for them to put on a short cycling race for charity today."

"Sure was. They get some practice and it's for a great cause." Mary nodded.

"Let's go, bring your camera, I'm sure you'll get some great shots."

"Oh, good idea, I'd love to get some in-motion shots. That photography class I've been taking has taught me so much. I'll meet you out front." Mary hurried down the hall towards her room.

Suzie walked out onto the front porch. On either side of her were two large, wooden rocking chairs. She and Mary often sat in them and enjoyed the view of the street beyond the parking lot. So many people walked to places in Garber that they usually had a chance to wave to each of their neighbors. Suzie went down to the yard and made sure Pilot had plenty of water to drink then stepped back onto the porch.

"All set." Mary stepped out with the camera hanging around her neck.

"Great, we can take the shortcut to the park." Suzie led the way down a narrow path that led through a small patch of woods between *Dune House* and the park. They emerged from the trees not far from the playground that was teeming with children.

"Oh, those sounds." Mary smiled as she drank in

the sight of the energetic kids running in all different directions. "I'll never think of them as anything but sweet."

"Sweet, in small doses." Suzie laughed, then shook her head as a shriek made her jump.

"Maybe." Mary grinned.

"If we get to the bridge we'll be able to see all of the cyclists come around the bend." Suzie grabbed Mary's hand and led her towards the nearby pedestrian bridge. It had been built a few months before to give people a safer way to cross the main road that led from Garber to Parish. It also connected two green spaces, a nature reserve, and a large recreation center and playground.

"It's nice to see no traffic on the road for once." Mary walked a little faster as they neared the bridge. "I hope we can catch them."

"Oh, here they come!" Suzie grinned as she grabbed Mary's hand and helped her up the steps. "We made it just in time."

As they walked up to the railing, the field of bikes had just rounded the bend. The bright colors of the cyclists' athletic gear flashed in the sunlight. The subtle whir of the bicycle wheels added to the buzz of excitement.

"Who is that in the lead?" Suzie peered down over the railing.

"Oh, it looks like Simon, and Michael is right behind him!" Mary grinned. "One of our very own guests. If he's doing this good now, then he's going to do great in the big race!"

"Michael's gaining on him." Suzie clapped her hands, then waved to a few other locals who had begun to gather on the bridge. As the group of riders began to approach the bridge, Michael pulled up right beside Simon. The two disappeared under the bridge.

"Hurry, we can see them on the other side." Mary turned, just as everyone else did on the bridge, and they managed to make it to the other side as a few cyclists came out. "What? Where are Michael and Simon?" Mary scanned the trickle of cyclists that emerged from under the bridge.

"Someone call an ambulance!" The shout came from under the bridge, followed by more shouts.

CHAPTER 2

"Call an ambulance!" The words echoed through Suzie's mind. She gasped, grabbed her phone, and made the call. She knew that there were EMTs close by in preparation for any accidents. After hanging up she joined the others as they rushed off the bridge to see what happened. Under the bridge, a crowd of cyclists had gathered around two abandoned bicycles.

Dazed by the sight of the bicycles, the sound of a shriek jolted Mary from her frozen state.

"Is someone hurt?" Mary stepped closer, with Suzie at her side.

"It's Simon." One of the other cyclists spoke up. "There's been a crash!"

"Simon, breathe buddy." Michael crouched

down beside him. "I know it hurts, just try to breathe. An ambulance is on its way."

"Oh, it hurts!" Simon groaned and grabbed his arm, which caused him to shriek again. "I think it's broken."

"It looks like it." Suzie frowned as she eyed his arm. It was bent in a way that it shouldn't have been.

"My son broke his arm once." Mary shook her head as she recalled the intensity of that moment. "I can't imagine pain like that."

"Everybody, back up a bit." Suzie shooed them away from Simon and Michael. "Give him some space to breathe. The paramedics will be here soon."

"Didn't you see me?" Simon gasped out as he stared fiercely at Michael. "I was right next to you! You slammed right into me!"

"I'm so sorry!" Michael frowned as he looked over at the mangled bicycles. "My wheel must have hit something slippery, I lost control, we were both going so fast." His voice trailed off as he looked back at Simon.

"Or you just wanted to win, that bad." Stuart stepped out of the crowd that had gathered near the bridge. Spectators, who had been watching the charity race, had heard quickly about the crash.

Stuart's anger was illustrated by every tensed muscle in his face. "You ran into him on purpose, didn't you?"

"No, of course not!" Michael stumbled back as Stuart approached him.

"His arm is broken, he's never going to be able to race now. I'm sure that's exactly what you wanted." Stuart's voice raised with every word he spoke.

"Take it easy." Suzie frowned as she looked between the two men. "The police and the ambulance will be here soon. Everything will get worked out."

"No, I'm not going to take it easy," Stuart snapped, then turned his attention on the crowd. "Who saw it? I know one of you must have. Who saw Michael crash into Simon?"

"Stuart, it's not true, I didn't do it on purpose." Michael backed away again as Stuart approached him. The two prowled in a slow circle, filled with the tension of what might happen at any second.

Suzie was about to step between them when sirens drowned out the argument. An ambulance, and Jason's car, squealed to a stop just beyond the bridge. As the paramedics hurried to tend to Simon, Jason jogged over to the scene as well.

"Are you hurt?" One of the paramedics looked over Michael.

"No, I'm fine." Michael waved her away.

"Yes, he's just fine. Because this wasn't a crash, it was an assassination," Stuart growled his words, then turned to Jason. "You need to arrest him, right now."

"Hold on just a second." Jason stared straight at Stuart. "It isn't up to you who I arrest. Deciding who, that is my job, not yours. I'd like you to take a step back until I can assess what happened here. Suzie?" He glanced at her. "What did you see?"

"She didn't see anything!" Stuart huffed. "She was on the bridge."

"We were." Suzie nodded. "They went under the bridge, and never came out on the other side. They were neck and neck."

"Too close for comfort, right Michael?" Stuart scowled. "You just had to make sure he didn't get ahead of you."

"Enough!" Michael shouted and started towards Stuart.

Jason stepped between them, and put one hand on Michael's chest.

"Calm down! We'll figure this out down at the

station." Jason's commanding tone silenced them both.

As the ambulance drove off with Simon in the back, Jason led Stuart and Michael to his patrol car. He instructed Stuart to sit in the front, and Michael to sit in the back.

"I'd hate to be trapped in that car with those two." Mary shivered at the thought. "I'm not sure that they'll ever stop arguing."

"Do you think Stuart is right?" Suzie looked over at Mary with a raised eyebrow. "What if Michael really did deliberately crash into him?"

"I suppose he could have, but I think it's more likely that the wheel did slide, like he claimed. With as fast as they were going, anything could have happened." Mary watched as the crowd began to disperse. "I'm guessing he will be tried in the court of popular opinion, however."

"Maybe." Suzie began to walk around beneath the bridge. She pulled out her phone and turned on the flashlight. As she pointed the beam towards the ground she studied every nuance of the pavement for any sign of a slick spot. "There is a small puddle, but I'm not sure that it would be enough to cause the tire to slip." She shone the flashlight on the tiny gathering of water.

"At those speeds, it's possible that it was enough." Mary eyed it closely. "But I don't see any tire marks on the pavement. I don't know who to believe. I'd rather think that it was an accident, and since we have no way to prove otherwise, I think we should stick to that."

"You're right." Suzie smiled as she looked up at her friend. "You're so level-headed. No need to look for a mystery where there isn't one."

"I have a mystery for you." Mary looked into her eyes as she smiled. "What are you going to wear to the event dinner tonight?"

"Good question." Suzie checked her phone. "Oh, and Paul can join me. I thought he'd think of an excuse to get out of it. You know how he is at these social events."

"Yes, and I also know he'd do just about anything to spend some time with you." Her eyes glowed with affection as she thought of Paul. "I'm so glad that you two found each other."

"Me, too." Suzie glanced in the direction of the docks. Her attention was often drawn there as she thought of Paul. She could recall the first time she met him, and how guarded he'd seemed. Perhaps she had come across the same way to him. Now, she couldn't imagine not looking forward to seeing him again.

As they walked back to *Dune House* together, the town was alive with gossip. Small groups of people stood knotted together deep in discussion. Snippets of their conversations floated through the air.

"I heard it was intentional."

"He broke his leg."

"He broke both of his arms."

"He broke both arms and both legs!"

The more extravagant the story became, the more concerned Suzie grew. If people were passing around these stories, she guessed that it wouldn't be long before they decided that Michael really was guilty of something. She hoped that it wouldn't turn into some kind of witch hunt.

"Jason needs to get to the bottom of this, and fast, or we might have a real uproar on our hands." Suzie shook her head as they passed a larger group of people, some locals mixed with some visiting athletes, who all seemed to be engaged in attacking Michael's character. She felt some relief when she reached *Dune House*, until she opened the door.

"You will release him right now, you had no reason to take him into custody." Jen shouted into her phone.

Suzie closed the door firmly behind Mary, then looked in Jen's direction.

Jen's gaze flitted towards her, but it did not stop her tirade on the phone.

"I don't care who you are, or what your credentials are, I'm coming down there and I expect Michael to be ready to go. He has training to do before the race, and as far as I'm concerned this qualifies as pure sabotage by the Garber police department. Do you have a problem with Michael because he's from Parish? Is that it?"

Charles started to walk into the entrance from the living room, but froze when he heard the shouting. He looked at Suzie and Mary, then turned and hurried back into the living room.

Mary gazed at Jen nervously. She'd heard stories about her being quite fierce when she wanted to be. When Jen hung up the phone she turned to face Suzie and Mary.

"Can you believe they actually took Michael to the police station? This is insane, everyone is going to think that he did something wrong." Jen flung her purse over her shoulder and gripped her keys so tight in her hand that her skin turned beet red.

"Just try to take a breath, Jen. The only reason Michael was taken to the police station is because he and Stuart were arguing over what happened to Simon. I'm sure everything has been straightened out by now." Suzie tried to keep her voice in a reasonable tone, but the woman's temper had her own nerves on edge.

"I don't care what the reason is, he had no right to do it. Excuse me." Jen pushed past them both to get out the door. As Suzie and Mary stared after her, she stormed down the steps and straight into the parking lot. The tires on her car squealed as she pulled out of the parking lot and onto the road.

"Jason isn't going to know what hit him." Mary tried to hide a quiet laugh.

"You're right about that." Suzie grinned. "I'm sure he can handle it, though. I'd better start getting ready for dinner. I'll be upstairs if you need me. It's a pity we couldn't both go tonight."

"Someone has to hold the fort." Mary smiled and headed for the living room. "I'm going to put my legs up for a bit."

As Suzie climbed the stairs to her room, she hoped that Jason knew what he was getting himself into. Was he prepared for such an angry coach? She knew that most coaches, and perhaps Jen in particular, took the race very seriously.

As Suzie showered she pushed the thoughts

from her mind, and instead focused on how much she would enjoy dinner with Paul. As she dressed she realized that they hadn't been on a real date in some time. Most of their time was spent on the beach, or relaxing on the porch of *Dune House*. That was just fine with her, she treasured the moments they shared together, enjoying each other's company and sharing their experiences, their interests, and their hopes for the future. But it would be nice to dress up a bit.

Suzie could remember a time when she never left the house without a full face of make-up, and her hair styled just right. It seemed so long ago, now. She'd traded in her fashion sense for beach-style comfort. Luckily, she still had a few nice dresses in the back of her closet. As she slipped on a black cocktail dress she felt as if she had stepped back through time. A flutter of excitement made her smile. She applied her make-up, styled her shoulder-length hair, which she dyed a brassy gold, then headed out of her bedroom.

A quick glance at the large clock on the wall in the kitchen revealed that Paul would be arriving in just a few minutes.

"Oh Suzie!" Mary gasped as she caught sight of her. "You look amazing!" She set down the plate she had been drying and walked over to her. "Sometimes I forget just how glamorous you can look."

"It's just smoke and mirrors." Suzie laughed, then gave her friend a hug. "I feel like I'm playing dress-up."

"You look fantastic." Mary hugged her in return, then glanced towards the door. "Paul's already on the porch."

"He is? He's early." Suzie laughed.

"He's eager." Mary winked at her. "You should see him out there in that suit prowling around. If you don't get out there soon, he might just change into jeans."

"He probably would." Suzie grinned. "Hey, call me if anything changes. If things get too busy, I can always come home."

"I'll be fine." Mary waved her off. "Go enjoy your evening."

"Thanks Mary." Suzie held her gaze for a moment, then headed for the front door. As she reached for the knob, she held her breath. It was a little silly to be nervous, she and Paul had been together for some time now, but still, there was that flutter. When she pulled the door open, he turned to face her. Dressed in a dark suit, paired with a white dress shirt, and a dark blue tie, she admired the way the colors accentuated his gray eyes, and the fit showed off his frame.

"Suzie, wow." He stared at her, his lips parted. "I mean, you look beautiful."

"Thanks." Suzie smiled at his awkward stammering. "You look pretty good yourself." She wrapped an arm around his neck and pulled him close for a light kiss. "I'm so glad I get to spend the evening with you."

"Me too." He tugged her closer for a deeper kiss.

She laughed as she pulled away.

"Now you're the one wearing lipstick." She used her thumb to wipe away a few smudges from his lips.

"I don't mind." Paul winked at her, then looped his arm through hers. "Are you sure you don't want to just take off for the evening?"

"Nervous about mingling, hmm?" Suzie grinned as they walked to his car. "Don't worry, you won't have to socialize too much. Everyone will be too busy talking about the race, and the crash between Michael and Simon."

"Oh, that was terrible, I heard that the poor boy broke both arms and legs." He frowned as he opened the passenger side door for her.

"You can't believe everything you hear." Suzie

shook her head as she climbed in. On the way to the diner she filled him in on what really happened. "I don't know for sure if his arm is broken, but it sure looked like it."

"Wow, that's quite a bit different from the story I heard. Do you think Michael did it on purpose?" He pulled into the diner that was already crowded with cars.

"I'm not sure, to be honest. It was perfect timing for them to crash under the bridge where the accident wouldn't be witnessed by the spectators, and the other cyclists were too busy focusing on the race to see what happened." Suzie stepped out of the car as he walked around to meet her. "It seems too perfect not to be planned, doesn't it? Or maybe I'm just being too suspicious about it."

"I guess the truth will come out soon enough." He wrapped his arm around hers. "You're going to protect me in there right?"

"I'll do my best." Suzie kissed his cheek.

CHAPTER 3

The diner had been transformed from a comfortable eatery to a fine dining experience. The booths were disguised by fine table-cloths, and the counter had been adorned with an assortment of silver serving dishes. Although the diner's classic charm was still visible, everything else had been dressed up for the evening, including the staff. Suzie smiled and waved at a few people she recognized, but the majority of the people in attendance were unfamiliar to her. Paul excused himself to get them both drinks, just as Jason walked towards her from the other side of the diner. His haggard expression was enough indication that he'd had quite the afternoon. He barely managed a smile as he reached her side.

"Are you still talking to me at least?"

"Of course I am." Suzie smiled. "Did Jen give you a hard time?"

"Oh, it wasn't just Jen. It was Jen, and Shelly, and Andrew. And even Charles got into it. He told me I was tainting the race by interfering with the competitors." He rolled his eyes and sighed. "I thought we might have some fireworks from all of the tension, but I didn't expect it to be like this."

"That must be difficult. How is Simon doing?" Suzie met Paul's eyes as he returned with their drinks. "Paul, Jason was just giving me an update on the situation we discussed."

"Ah." Paul raised his thick eyebrows. "I bet you're having a blast with all of it."

"Definitely." Jason grimaced. "Simon is going to be okay. It was a clean break and should heal well. But of course he can't be in the race, which has Stuart livid. He demanded I order an investigation of the crime scene. When I pointed out that there was no crime, he threatened me with his high-powered lawyers." He pressed his fingertips against his forehead. "I don't think there's much chance of this dying down too soon. Luckily the race is in a couple of days, and by the end of the weekend, everyone will be gone, and hopefully all of this will be forgotten."

"So, you don't think that Michael did it on purpose?" Paul took a sip of his drink.

"There's no evidence to prove that. Michael has been very cooperative and seemed genuinely remorseful. Without anything to go on, I can't exactly start an investigation. I told Stuart if he brings me some solid evidence, then I will certainly investigate it. Meanwhile, Jen was threatening to have me fired over my obvious favoritism, even though I released Michael." Jason held up his hands in surrender. "I'm over all of it."

"Aw relax, sweetheart." Summer rubbed his shoulders as she walked up behind him. "This is supposed to be a party, remember? Come dance with me." She winked at Suzie and Paul, before she tugged Jason out onto the small dance floor in the middle of the room.

"Poor kid." Paul frowned. "He's in over his head on this one."

"He's right though, this will all blow over by next week. At least he won't have to deal with most of these people again after that." Suzie sipped her drink and smiled at the sweet taste. "Mango, my favorite."

"Of course." He gazed into her eyes. "Do you want to dance?"

"Really?" She grinned. "You wouldn't mind?"

"Of course not. I'd be honored." Paul took her drink from her hand, then set it and his own on a nearby table. As he led her out onto the dance floor, Suzie was certain that her night couldn't get any better.

As the night continued on, the drinks continued to flow. Suzie noticed Stuart's arrival, and Michael's absence. Although, Jen was present, along with the rest of the team from Parish, there was no sign of Michael. The conversation steered specifically away from Simon and Michael, as if people had been warned not to discuss it. However, the tension still rippled throughout the diner. As she broke away from Paul to replenish their drinks, Suzie's attention was drawn towards a raised voice. It only took her a moment to recognize Stuart, and the race organizer, Alana. They stood practically toe to toe, not far from the beverage table. As she began to assess the situation, it became even more volatile. Stuart's body language clearly indicated frustration, while Alana shied back from his aggression. Without a second thought Suzie began to gravitate towards them. She had the sense that things could get out of hand very quickly if they were allowed to escalate. As she neared them, she could hear more clearly what the argument was about.

"I want to know exactly what is going to happen to Michael. There had better be consequences, severe ones." Stuart's jaw rippled with anger.

"At this time, we are still reviewing the incident." Alana gazed back at him with thinly veiled impatience. "If anything is found I will let you know."

"You're not doing enough! Michael did this on purpose! Simon could have been killed! Michael should be disqualified, if not arrested!" Stuart swung his hand through the air to punctuate each of his words. "I'm telling you right now, if something isn't done then I am going to rally the other athletes to protest. Then you won't even have a race, will you?"

"Stuart, you need to calm down." Alana's shoulders tensed, and her voice hardened. "And keep your voice down! Even Simon says it was an accident."

"Of course, Simon says that. He's a kind person. He believes that people are good. But it's not true. I know that Michael ran into him on purpose. He wanted to take out the competition. Without Simon he knows that our team doesn't have a chance to win, and it's too late now to get someone else to join in." Stuart stabbed a finger in the direction of her face. "Either you do something about this, or I will, that's all there is to say about it."

As Stuart spun on his heel and stormed away, Suzie stepped forward to Alana's side.

"Are you all right? He seemed pretty upset." Suzie placed her hand lightly on the woman's elbow, and felt a tremor there.

"He's always upset about something." Alana narrowed her eyes, then looked towards Suzie with a gentle smile. "He'll blow off steam the way he usually does, with a wild party, and then he'll be fine again. I'm telling you, if he would just clean up his act he would be an amazing talent."

"He struggles a bit with his fame, hmm?" Suzie looked off in the direction of Stuart as he headed for the door of the diner.

"More than a bit. He was so young when he first got into national sports. Honestly, I feel bad for him. His mother wasn't exactly interested in anything other than the money he could make for her." Alana crossed her arms. "But that doesn't excuse this kind of behavior. He's toxic." She sneered in his direction, then walked off towards the buffet table.

Suzie recalled Simon's mention of Stuart's mother being in town, and wondered if Alana was right about her. If so, Stuart had likely led a very lonely life.

～

*A*fter a long evening, Paul dropped Suzie off at *Dune House*. She noticed that Wes' car wasn't in the parking lot, and assumed that he'd already gone home. Inside the house was quiet. Pilot must have already gone to bed with Mary. Suzie crept up the stairs to her room and barely had enough energy to wash off her make-up and change into a nightgown before she collapsed on the bed.

What seemed like moments later, insistent pounding on the door made Suzie jolt out of sleep. Sluggish, and uncertain what was reality and what was dream, she stumbled out of her bed. The pounding continued. She recognized the sound of Pilot barking. He never barked in the middle of the night. Something had him spooked. As her mind spun she became aware that all of the guests would be woken up by the noise. Who could it be? Had someone gone out and forgotten their key? But the pounding was far too loud for that. It seemed to shake the entire house, though she knew that wasn't possible. As she made her way to the hallway, and continued down the stairs, she heard shuffling below her.

"Mary? Is that you?" Suzie reached the bottom of the stairs and spotted Mary as she stepped into the kitchen.

"What is going on?" Mary's eyes widened as she clutched her robe around her. "It's not even seven yet. Who could it be?"

"I don't know, but we're going to have to find out." Suzie eyed the door as the pounding began again.

Pilot continued to bark, to the point that his whole body bounced with every sound he made. He stood a few feet from the door, his nails clicking and sliding against the hardwood floor as he moved back and forth anxiously.

Suzie walked up to the door, with Mary a few steps behind. As Mary attempted to soothe Pilot, Suzie reached for the door. The knob squeaked as she turned it, then eased the door open. Jason stood on the other side, along with several uniformed officers.

"Suzie, I'm sorry about this, but we have a warrant to search *Dune House*. You and everyone inside need to allow access to every room." The hint of apology in his eyes did nothing to soften the authority in his voice.

"I don't understand?" Suzie stared at him and briefly wondered if she might still be sleeping. "A warrant? But why? What's happened, Jason?"

"There isn't time to discuss it at the moment, but I need a list of everyone who is staying here." Jason brushed past her, into the house. Behind him, the officers filed in. "No one is to leave the property, understand?" He looked back over his shoulder at her. "I have officers along the perimeter."

"Yes, I think so." She looked over at Mary, who seemed just as confused.

Once Pilot saw Jason, he stopped barking and started panting. He tried to lick Jason's hand, but Jason used it to point out which direction he wanted each officer to go in.

"Check each room, be polite about it, but insist everyone leave their rooms so that we can search them. You can gather the guests in the living room for now. We'll need to question each one." Jason grabbed the shoulder of one officer who started for the stairs. "Be polite." He repeated, this time more sternly.

The officer nodded, then headed up the stairs.

"Jason, wait a minute." Mary frowned as she watched two officers pass her and head up the stairs in the living room. "Most of our guests are still sleeping, you're going to scare them."

"There isn't time for niceties, Mary." His sharp tone surprised them both.

"Jason —" Suzie began.

"Suzie, I'm sorry. You have to understand this is a very serious investigation." Jason glanced over his shoulder, then lowered his voice. "I don't want to cause panic, but we found Stuart Pike dead this morning, floating in the water near the docks."

"Oh no!" Suzie gasped as she tried to decide whether the news could be true. Of course, Jason wouldn't lie to her, but the horror of the truth was worse than believing her cousin had briefly lost his senses. "Was it some kind of accident?"

"No, it was no accident. He was found wrapped in a bedsheet, a sheet with *Dune House* printed on the corner." Jason locked eyes with Suzie, his expression rigid and determined. "Which leads us to believe that someone here may have committed the crime. That's why the warrant was approved, and why we had to execute the search without warning. I hope you can understand." His tone softened some.

"Someone here?" Mary sputtered, then grabbed Suzie's arm. "Are you hearing this?"

"I am." Suzie finally felt fully awake, but she wished she didn't. Her stomach twisted with grief for the loss of life, and also fear at the idea that someone under her roof had done such a terrible thing. "But it must be some kind of mistake."

"I'm afraid at this point, it is the only evidence we have to go on. We can't risk losing evidence by delaying the search. I know this is very inconvenient for both of you, but it has to happen." Jason adjusted his radio on his hip, then looked back at Suzie. "I need that list, of every guest currently staying here, and anyone else who has been on the property within the past let's say, forty-eight hours. Don't leave anyone out."

"I'll do my best." Suzie made her way over to the front desk, with Mary right behind her.

"Can you believe this?" Mary shook her head, her eyes wide and dazed. "How could something like this happen?"

"I don't know. But I'm going to do whatever I can to help Jason. Yes, we may have some angry guests, but nothing is more important than finding out what happened to Stuart." Her fingers flew across the keys as she began to create a list of the guests.

"Yes, you're right of course." Mary closed her eyes. "Let's see, Wes was here last night. Alana stopped by earlier in the day, remember?"

"Yes, Wes and Alana. Anyone else? Did the gardener come by?" Suzie pursed her lips as she tried to remember.

"No, he was out on Monday. No one else has been here other than the guests, and well Jason." Mary shrugged. "I suppose he doesn't need himself added to the list."

"Good, I think we have everyone." Suzie hit the key to print the list, then walked over to the printer. "I hope this will help him."

"Me too. I guess there's no way this could be anything but a homicide. Most people don't wrap themselves up in a sheet and then drown." Mary winced at her own words. "If that's even how he died."

"I'm sure we'll find out more as the day progresses, but for now Jason needs to focus on the task at hand." Suzie watched as several of the guests descended the stairs, escorted by police officers. The team from out of state came down the stairs first. They looked worried, but not angry. They were then followed a few seconds later by Jen, who was looking quite angry, followed by Andrew and Shelly. That left only Charles and Michael. Her heart flipped as she wondered if perhaps Michael had something to do with this. Stuart and Michael had been arguing quite a bit. But could Michael be capable of murder? Suzie wasn't sure if she believed that. Then again, she didn't think any of the guests were capable of murder. She also knew next to nothing about them. Other than what she had heard about them during their stay, she hadn't discovered anything more about them.

"I'm going to see if it's okay to make coffee. If we all must go through this, coffee will help." Mary headed for the kitchen, where one of the officers lingered, monitoring both the hallway and the back door.

As Suzie picked up the list from the printer she spotted Jason headed in her direction. She braced herself for what he might have already discovered.

CHAPTER 4

It seemed to Suzie that every step Jason took to cross the room was a heavy one. Suzie didn't realize until he stopped, that he had been walking in time with the thud of her heartbeats. Once he met her eyes, she could tell that he didn't know much more.

"I have your list." Suzie offered it to him.

"Thanks. Is everyone staying here accounted for?" Jason glanced over the list. "We've rounded everyone up into the living room."

"I saw Ali, Carter, Sam, Jen, Shelly, and Andrew. What about Charles and Michael?" She peered past him, towards the living room.

"Charles is in there, but not Michael. He's not in any of the rooms upstairs either." Jason crossed his arms as he narrowed his eyes. "I certainly know that he and Stuart were not on friendly terms. Did you see him last night?"

"Uh, actually I didn't see anyone when I got home. I just assumed that everyone was asleep or still out. Mary?" Suzie called out to her in the kitchen. "Can you join us?"

"Sure." Mary walked over to Jason with a mug of coffee. "I thought you might like this."

"Thanks Mary." He spared her a small smile as he took the mug.

"Did you see Michael before you locked up last night?" Suzie felt her muscles tense. She knew at this point, Michael was a prime suspect.

"No, I didn't. I assumed he was staying late at the dinner." Mary shrugged.

"He wasn't at the dinner." Suzie frowned. "I would have noticed him there."

"Yes, I didn't see him, either." Jason sighed. "I guess that means he didn't come back last night."

"Not necessarily." Mary shook her head. "He could have come in and I just didn't notice. Maybe he went out early this morning. We can't just assume that he didn't come back at all."

"No, we can't. But it's a good place to start."

Jason pulled out his radio and barked a command into it. "We'll find him."

"Find who?" Jen stepped up to the front desk, her eyes narrowed. "Are you talking about Michael?"

Suzie bristled at the tone of Jen's voice, and she could tell that Jason didn't appreciate it either, by the way he cut his eyes in her direction.

"I asked you to stay in the living room." Jason tipped his head towards it. "Please take a seat."

"Respectfully, no." Jen stood her ground as she locked eyes with Jason. "If you're trying to pin this on Michael, I'm not going to let that happen."

"No one is trying to pin anything on anyone. Do you know where Michael is at the moment?" Jason turned to fully face her. "He wasn't in his room, and doesn't appear to be on the property."

"He should have been in his room." Jen's expression flickered with concern for a moment, then hardened. "I spoke to him on the phone last night. Just before I went to bed. He told me he was going to come back and go to sleep. I had warned him not to go to the dinner, because I knew that everyone would attack him for his involvement in Simon's accident. Instead, he went for a bicycle ride. I'm sure that's what he's doing now. He probably got up early to train, since he missed out on so much time yesterday, thanks to you." She frowned as she looked into Jason's eyes. "I can tell you he had nothing to do with any of this."

"You seem pretty confident about that, even though you have no idea where he is right now." Jason held her gaze. "Maybe you should call him, ask him to come back here?"

"No." Jen took a step back. "If you want him, you find him." She turned and walked back into the living room.

"Stellar cooperation." Jason's lips drew into a thin, straight line.

"No, she's not being very cooperative." Suzie bit into her bottom lip. "Take it one step at a time, Jason."

"Oh, I intend to." He made a note on the list he held. "Once we find Michael we should know a bit more. Until then, I'm afraid we're going to have to do a thorough search of the entire house."

"Even our rooms?" Mary frowned.

"I'm sorry, yes. We have to make sure that all the bases are covered. I'll do my best to monitor the search and make sure that nothing is damaged or left in a mess. All right?" Jason looked between them, then took a deep breath. "I know this is hard on both of you, I wish there was another way."

"It's okay." Suzie patted his arm. "Don't worry about it, Jason. Just do your job."

"She's right." Mary nodded and offered him a warm smile. "The important thing is that you find out the truth. Oh Jason, this is all so awful. How could one of our sheets have been found at the scene? Did someone really steal one? Were there any sheets missing from the beds?"

"Not that we've seen so far. Do you know how many sheets should be in the linen closet?"

"No, not exactly." Mary shook her head.

"Okay. We're going to do our best to figure this out. However. I think it's very unlikely that someone just walked in off the street and stole one." Jason swept his gaze over the people gathered in the living room. "As far as I'm concerned every one of your guests is a main suspect at the moment, at least until I can clear them." He glanced at his watch, then frowned. "It's seven-thirty, where could Michael be?"

"I hope he's okay. Like Jen said, he might be out training." Suzie shook her head as she looked over the worried faces assembled in the living room.

"He's quite an athlete. But I suppose there won't be a race tomorrow."

"Yes, he is, I've seen him in action. But he also had that bang-up with Simon yesterday, and Stuart was angling for him to be disqualified." He glanced over the list again, then added it to the folder in his hand. "Thanks for being so cooperative, Suzie, Mary. I know it's not easy for you to have *Dune House* invaded like this."

"The part that isn't easy is accepting that Stuart is dead." Suzie sighed. "I should check with Paul, he might have seen or noticed something at the docks this morning. I mean, someone had to have seen something, right?"

"Summer's best guess at the moment is that Stuart was killed around three-thirty, and put into the water by four. He didn't drown, Suzie. That's just how the killer tried to dispose of his body. There was a heavy rock that he was tied to with a rope, but the rope came loose. Since all fishing near the docks is banned during the event I doubt that any of the fishermen were awake, or that many were on their boats when this happened. But I plan to have some officers question everyone that was nearby." He pulled his hat off and ran his hand back through his red hair. "I can't believe this happened either, Suzie. It was supposed to be such a wonderful weekend."

"I know you knew Stuart." Suzie looked into his eyes. "I know you admired him."

"We didn't know each other well. I'd seen him at a few events. But still, it's a shock." Jason shook his head. "I hope I can get to the bottom of this, and fast. The media is going to be all over this in no time."

"I know it." Suzie grimaced.

"That won't be fun." Mary felt some tension build in her chest. "I think I need to get some air. Is that okay? For me to go outside?"

"Of course, it is." He nodded.

"I'll join you." Suzie called Pilot to her side. "Let's go, boy."

In the living room Suzie could hear Jen's voice raising again. She guessed she was arguing with one of the officers interviewing her. She held the door for Mary and Pilot, then pulled the door shut behind her.

The warm air coated Mary's skin, as she leaned against the railing and tried to catch her breath. Muggy, that was the way to describe it. Thick and heated. Mary couldn't get her heart to slow down. She was anxious about what the police officers were doing inside, and anxious about how the guests felt as they were interviewed in the living room, and anxious about what happened to Stuart.

"Mary, are you okay?" Suzie rubbed her hand along Mary's shoulder.

"I will be." Mary straightened her shoulders. "I just don't know what to think about Stuart's death. Mostly, how *Dune House* could have been involved. I hate the thought that someone staying with us could have done something like this." She met Suzie's eyes. "Do you think it was someone here?"

"I'm not sure. My first instinct is to say no, but then, I could easily be wrong. We both know that Jen has a temper, and that she was quite angry with Stuart. Then there is Michael, who could easily be involved. Not to mention the other two members of the Parish team and the team from out of state, any one of them could have decided to hurt Stuart. I don't want to think it, no, but Jason is right, everyone at *Dune House* is a suspect." Suzie took a deep breath, then looked back towards the house. "I wish it wasn't true, but wishing doesn't change it."

"No, it doesn't." Mary frowned as she stared at the house. "How long do you think it will take before they complete the search?" She wrung her hands as she paced back and forth along the front porch.

"I'm not sure." Suzie couldn't tear her eyes away from the front door. It was so odd to think of the police officers walking through each room, hunting for evidence of a murder that she still couldn't believe happened. "My guess is they're going to go through all of the rooms thoroughly, and likely check all of the bedding. Whatever Jason needs to do, to find the truth."

"Suzie!" Paul ran up the beach from the direction of the docks. He waved to her as he approached.

"Paul." Suzie smiled at the sight of him. Just his presence offered her some comfort. She could remember a time when she held back in their relationship, when she doubted that she could ever want to be close to someone. But he'd changed that about her, just by being who he was.

"Are you two okay?" Paul mounted the steps to the porch. "I just heard what happened. I would have been here sooner, but I was being questioned." He narrowed his eyes as he saw a police officer step out through the door, then head down the steps past him. "Are they searching *Dune House*?"

"Yes." Suzie took his hand. "Because of how Stuart was found."

"How he was found?" He looked between them, confused.

"He was wrapped up in one of our bedsheets," Mary whispered her words, but her voice still trembled under the weight of them.

"So, they think someone staying here was involved?" His eyes widened.

"Yes." Suzie nodded. "I still haven't quite wrapped my head around it. Someone here might have done it?"

"We don't know that's what happened, yet." Paul wrapped his arm around her shoulders. "The investigation is just getting started."

"Did you see anything this morning, Paul?" Suzie locked eyes with him. "Anything around the docks? Did you hear anything?"

"I don't think so." He frowned. "It was quiet, with no fishing. I just remember thinking that it was peaceful."

"What about Michael? Did you see any sign of him? Maybe on your way here?" Suzie's heart pounded with urgency.

"No, I didn't see him. But I did see a bike laying in the sand." He tipped his head back in the direction that he came. "About halfway between the docks and here."

"You did?" Suzie's eyes widened. "Maybe it's Michael's."

"We should tell Jason." Mary started for the door, but it swung open before she could reach it. Jason stepped outside, his expression grim.

"What did you find?" Suzie asked.

"Nothing yet. I've spoken to all of the guests, but one." He glanced at his tablet. "Michael Whittel."

"He's not back, yet." Suzie pulled away from Paul as she met Jason's eyes. "But Paul spotted a bicycle on the beach not far from here. It could be Michael's."

"Thanks, I'll have someone check it out." Jason stuck his head back into the house and summoned an officer.

"I can show him where, if you'd like." Paul nodded to Jason.

"Sure, thanks." Jason watched as the officer and Paul walked off together. Then he turned back to Mary and Suzie. "I've had someone out looking for Michael, and they haven't found him yet. With his conflict with Stuart, I need to speak to him, he might be involved in the murder, or even hurt." Jason scanned the beach, then looked back at them both. "If you see him or hear from him you need to contact me right away." His tone grew stern as he studied each of them in turn. "Immediately, understand?"

"Yes, of course." Mary frowned.

"The moment we hear of anything we'll tell you." Suzie searched his fatigued expression. "He insisted the crash was an accident, Jason. I'm not saying that he didn't do it, but I think there could be other possibilities."

"Trust me, I'm considering them. The search is complete. We couldn't find any sheets missing from the rooms, but that doesn't mean they aren't missing from the linen closet. A few officers will remain to keep a lookout for Michael. I will keep you up to date." As he headed down the steps of the porch, Mary moved closer to Suzie.

"Do you think he's doing okay?" Mary stared after Jason.

"I think he's determined to solve this murder. I hope that he keeps an open mind about Michael. I just can't imagine him doing this." Suzie looked over at Mary. "Not that we know him that well, but he seemed so shaken yesterday when he hit Simon. He seemed upset that he had caused him harm."

"No, we don't know him well, but you're right,

from the interaction I had with him I didn't get the feeling of him being a dangerous man. Sometimes people can put on a good show, kind one minute, and vicious the next." Mary clucked her tongue. "There's no way to know for sure. But Jason will get to the bottom of it. We probably have quite a mess to clean up in there."

"Yes, we'd better get to it. I'm sure everyone will be pretty upset, too. We should make sure there's some food out, it's past breakfast now." Suzie held open the door to *Dune House*. It seemed strange to discuss breakfast, as if it was any other day, and yet it was the only thing she could focus on.

"Absolutely." Mary took a deep breath, straightened her shoulders, then walked through the door.

Michael's teammates, Shelly and Andrew, along with Charles were knotted together in the living room. Jen was nowhere in sight.

As Suzie and Mary stepped into the living room, Charles stood up.

"I've called Alana. I made sure she knew what was going on here. My guess is the race will be called off. The police said we're not allowed to leave town, so I suppose I will stay here. But if you let that murderer back into this house—"

"He's not a murderer!" Shelly jumped to her feet.

"Shelly." Andrew stood up and grabbed her by the arm. "Let's go for a walk." He steered her towards the door, with the familiarity and concern that hinted at a romantic relationship between them.

"I can't kick Michael out, let's just see what happens with the investigation." Suzie cleared her throat. "You are welcome to stay, Charles."

"I don't have any other choice really, do I?" He headed for the stairs.

As Suzie and Mary were left alone in the living room, the two women gazed at each other.

"I guess no one's hungry," Mary mumbled, then began to pick up some books that had been knocked from the bookshelf.

CHAPTER 5

*S*ilence covered all of *Dune House* like a heavy blanket. Once Suzie and Mary had everything straightened up in the rooms, they met out on the deck.

"I feel like I need fresh air." Mary shook her head. "It's too tense in there?"

"I agree. I think the only thing that will ease the tension is finding out what happened to Stuart. Jason is going to have his hands full with all of these suspects to sort through. I don't think it would hurt anything to give him a helping hand." Suzie pulled out her phone. "We already know that Stuart was pretty well-known. The only thing that ties his death to *Dune House* is the sheet he was wrapped in. With his arrogance and behavior, I'm guessing he's made quite a few enemies over the years." As she began to sort through recent photographs posted of Stuart, she frowned. "As of now we know that Michael was not at the dinner last night, he was told not to be there. But Stuart was, and he made quite a scene during an argument with Alana. I'm sure everyone in the diner heard it. I think the people at the diner should be suspects as well."

"I don't think we should overlook Jen either." Mary crossed her arms as she peered at Suzie's phone. "She was so angry at the idea of Michael being accused."

"Maybe she had a confrontation with Stuart, and it got out of hand."

"Maybe, but why would she have the sheet? That aspect of this makes it seem premeditated. Most people don't walk around with a sheet." Mary frowned.

"Unfortunately, I agree, and that leads me to suspect that it's possible Stuart was killed somewhere on this property. If it was Jen, she might have panicked, and grabbed a sheet from the linen closet, seeing as it looks like none were missing from the guests' beds." Suzie winced at the thought. "Jason said he was likely killed in the very early hours of this morning. Which means all of this could have unfolded right here, while we were sleeping." She tucked her phone back into her pocket. "It's horrible to think it, but at the moment it makes the most sense. Of course, we can't accuse Jen of murder based on her having a temper, can we?"

"No, we certainly can't." When a car door slammed Mary turned towards the parking lot. "Oh, Wes is here." She smiled.

"Go and talk to him, I'm going to open the windows in the house and see if I can get some fresh air flowing." Suzie smiled at Mary, then stepped into the house.

"Mary, I was going to call first, but I was just around the corner. I hope I didn't interrupt." Wes ascended the steps onto the porch.

"No, I think Suzie just wanted to give us some time alone together." Mary hugged him. As his arms encircled her, he tightened them, even when she started to pull away.

"I heard what happened." He ran his hand down her back. "Are you okay?"

"It's terrible, Wes." Mary sighed.

"Yes, it is." He kissed her forehead. "I'm sure Jason will solve this quickly. My department is working with him as we speak."

"I'm glad. The sooner this is solved, the better it

is for everyone." Mary pulled back and took a breath. "Suzie and I were just talking about the possibility that Jen had something to do with it. But I don't know."

"Jen." He nodded. "I know of her, she's got a reputation for causing trouble, but nothing like this."

"Oh my, I wonder if anyone has told his mother." Mary frowned. "Do you know if anyone has?"

"His mother?" Wes studied her. "I'm sure that Jason has reached out to his next of kin."

"But she's here, she's in town. Simon said so yesterday." She tried to recall his exact words. "I think there was some kind of issue between her and Stuart, because he didn't seem happy to know that she was in town. But whatever the issue might have been, she deserves to know what's happened."

"Okay. I'll find out, and if no one has been able to reach her, then I will find her." He looked into her eyes. "Why don't you let the police deal with this and you and I spend the day out together? By the time we come home, hopefully all of this will be solved." He smiled. "Let me try and take your mind off all this."

"I don't know." Mary frowned. "I think it's best if I stay here, our guests may need me."

"Just an hour then." He tugged her gently towards the steps. "That's all I'm asking. Just some time for you and me, away from all of this."

"Wes?" Mary eyed him for a moment. "What is this really about? You're never one to shy away from an investigation. You're an amazing detective, what could stop you from wanting to solve this?"

"And you say I'm the detective?" Wes smiled some as he tucked a few strands of her hair behind her ear. "Yes, I am trying to steer you away from this investigation. But I have a good reason for that." He searched her eyes.

"Wes, I need more of an explanation than just that you have a good reason. I need to know what the reason is." Mary took his hands in hers. "Can't you tell me what's going on?"

"Not just yet. You're right. I'm conducting my own investigation. But at the moment, it is very delicate, and dangerous. I can't tell you about it." His phone beeped with a message. He looked from his phone to Mary. "I have to go. Maybe we could discuss this more later?"

"Sure." She nodded and met his lips for a quick kiss.

As he walked away, she was confused. What was he keeping from her. She decided that the best thing to do was distract herself. She needed some things from the store for the guests. She stuck her head inside the house, grabbed her keys from the key hooks near the door, and called out to Suzie. "I'm going out for a bit! I'm going to the store. Text me if you remember anything we forgot off the list."

"All right, tell Wes I say hi!" Suzie called back.

~

*T*here were many reasons for Suzie to remain in her room. She could use some rest after being woken up so early. She had a lot of thoughts to sort through. In general, it seemed like a good day to stay inside. However, she couldn't. The restlessness that brewed in her was impossible to ignore. Not long after Mary left, she decided to take a drive to the hospital and pay a visit to Simon. She had no idea whether she would even be allowed to see him, but she thought he would be the one to give her the best and most recent information about Stuart. They seemed to be quite close. Although she didn't know much about either man, she did know that Stuart had been quite protective of Simon when he was hurt. That kind of protectiveness didn't just come from a brief friendship. It was born of something deeper.

When Suzie arrived at the hospital, she noticed some reporters outside. She guessed that they were there to talk about Stuart, and that his body had likely originally been brought to the hospital. However, she couldn't be certain, as she hurried past them without listening in to the reports. Once inside the hospital, she headed for the front desk. She was about to ask about seeing Simon, when she heard his voice not far behind her. She turned and saw him being wheeled towards the door.

"I'm so sorry about this, Simon." Alana sighed as she pushed him towards the exit. "I know it has to be such a shock to you. Now remember, when the reporters ask you their questions, just keep it short, and focus on the positive."

"The positive?" Simon looked up at her. "Alana, there is nothing positive about any of this. I can't believe that Stuart is dead. Who would do something like this?"

"I'm afraid I can't answer that, but you'll need to speak with the police as well. Perhaps they can give you some idea of who killed him. For now, I need you to focus on the task at hand. These reporters have been waiting to speak with you." Alana glanced over her shoulder at the hospital staff, then turned back to the automatic doors. "Are you ready?"

"I guess. I just don't know what I'm supposed to say." He looked around him, as if seeking some kind of direction.

When his eyes landed on Suzie, she began to walk towards him.

"Hey. Suzie, right?" Simon smiled as he met her eyes. "You were there yesterday when I crashed on my bike."

"Yes, I was." She smiled in return. "Actually, I came here to see how you were doing. I'm glad to see that you're being released."

"Yes." He glanced down at his arm, which was in a sling. "I still have to get my cast on, but the doctors are waiting for the swelling to go down. I guess I'm out of luck." He closed his eyes, then shook his head. "Listen to me complaining about my arm when Stuart is dead. I'm sorry, I'm still having a hard time believing it."

"I understand." Suzie studied his youthful features and guessed he wasn't more than twenty. "I'm so sorry for your loss, Simon. I know that you were close to Stuart."

"Yes." His chin trembled.

"It's okay, Simon." Alana rubbed his shoulder. "I know it's hard right now, but you will be able to move past this. You still have an amazing career ahead of you."

"Enough." He sighed. "I don't want to even think about my career right now." He brushed Alana's hand away. "Why do I have to talk to these reporters anyway? Can't you just send them away?"

"I can if that's what you really want, Simon. But I thought you might want to say something about Stuart. It's best to give your reaction now, and be done with it, otherwise these reporters will hound you. Trust me, they've been hunting me down all morning."

"I'm sorry to hear that." Suzie frowned. "If you'd like I could get some police officers to escort you both out of the hospital."

"No thanks." Alana locked eyes with her. "I can handle this. The media knows that Stuart is dead, but it hasn't been released that he was murdered. The police asked to try and keep it out of the press for the moment. I've already announced that the race was canceled, but I guess some fans are hoping that we might just reschedule."

"You can't. Not without Stuart." Simon winced. "I can't even imagine doing this race without him."

"I haven't decided yet." Alana tightened her grip on the wheelchair handles.

"Listen Simon, you don't have to do anything you don't want to do. There's a rear exit from the hospital, I can show you where it is." Suzie looked up at Alana. "Do you want to do that?"

"No, I think it's better if he speaks now. If he holds back, it could create a scandal. Everyone will want to know why Stuart's best friend doesn't have anything to say." Alana shrugged as she began to roll him forward again. "It's entirely up to you, Simon, but I am speaking from experience when I say I've seen careers ruined from less. I was hoping you'd be able to compete next year."

"She's right." Simon shifted in the wheelchair, then frowned. "Besides, I owe it to Stuart to speak up for him. I keep thinking if I had just been there, instead of in the hospital, maybe I could have done something to protect him."

"You can't blame yourself, Simon. None of this was your fault." Suzie walked beside him as Alana began to roll him out through the doors. "But had you noticed him having a tough time with anyone since he'd arrived in Garber?"

"Not really, no. His spoiled behavior caused some annoyance, but that happened wherever we went. I wish I knew more, but that's all I know. If I knew who did this, I would be reporting it, right this second. Poor Stuart." Simon rubbed his hand across his face. "I never, never thought something like this would happen to him. It was like he was untouchable."

"It's a lot to take in." Alana glanced in the direction of the gathered reporters. "Are you ready, Simon?"

"Yes. I guess so." He looked up at Suzie one more time. "You know, he wasn't a terrible person. Not really. He just didn't have a lot to start with." He held her gaze as Alana rolled him through the doors.

Suzie stared after him, uncertain of what to make of what he said. Had Stuart come from poor beginnings? She suddenly recalled his reaction to Simon mentioning that he'd seen his mother in town. She couldn't help but wonder if anyone had notified her. As she slipped past the reporters and headed back to her car, she decided she would check in with Jason. She wanted to be sure that he knew about Stuart's mother being in town.

As Suzie pulled out of the parking lot, she looked back to see the flashes of the cameras. The reporters had surrounded Simon, but she could see

Alana's blonde hair shining in the sunlight. She'd made sure she was part of the spotlight. Was that good marketing, or did she really want to protect Simon's career? As the race organizer she imagined that she and her business stood to lose a lot due to the race being canceled, but she didn't seem to be too concerned about it. Maybe she was just putting on a brave face for Simon's sake. As Suzie drove towards the police station, she prepared for what she might encounter there. Had Jason managed to track down Michael yet?

CHAPTER 6

*M*ary drove towards the shops. She needed to pick up some vegetables and so she headed to the produce market in Parish. Although, it was a bit of a drive it had the best deals and she was planning on buying quite a few things. It was in a small outdoor mall, with an assortment of entertainment options. As she drove down the road she noticed Wes' car in front of her. He was headed in the opposite direction to his house and the Parish police station. She followed after him as he was headed in the direction of the shop. But after a few more minutes she saw him turn into the parking lot of a small bar. It was just late enough for it to be open, but it surprised her to see him stop there. Wes wasn't much of a drinker, and she couldn't imagine him leaving her side to have a few beers.

Mary continued past the bar, and pulled into the building beside it. It contained some shops including the small produce market. She parked along the side so that he wouldn't recognize her SUV. For a moment she considered just going into the shop. There was likely nothing for her to find, and perhaps she didn't really want to know what he was up to. But her curiosity was impossible to ignore. She climbed out of the SUV and crossed the distance between the two parking lots. As she watched from the corner of the building, Wes remained in his car. A few minutes later a car pulled up one space away from his. She couldn't quite see who was inside of it. After a few more minutes passed, Wes stepped out of the car. He walked over to the other one. He paused beside the passenger side door, then opened it, and sat down inside.

Shocked to see this, Mary crept a little farther out from the corner of the building. Who was he in the car with? Why did it seem so strange and secretive? Was she imagining that there was more to it than there was? She squinted at the windshield in an attempt to discover who was inside. But the sun glare on it was just enough to prevent her from being able to see inside. As seconds slipped by her mind ran wild with the possibilities of what might be happening inside the car. Why had they met in the car? The bar was right there, obviously they did not want to be seen for some reason. Which meant that whatever they were discussing had to be quite important.

Just as Mary was about to dare to creep closer to the car, the passenger side door opened, and Wes stepped out. He turned back, leaned into the car, and said something she couldn't hear. Then he closed the door and walked over to his car and got in. Though he pulled away, the other car remained in the parking spot. She was tempted to follow him, but was too curious about who might be in the car to walk away. As she watched, the driver's side door opened, and a woman stepped out. Mary didn't recognize her, but she was quite beautiful. Slender, with long, black hair, and just enough lines on her face to indicate they were about the same age. As she watched, the woman walked into the bar.

Quick hurt sparked within Mary. Wes was meeting with a woman? It was hard not to jump to the conclusion that he had found someone he enjoyed spending time with more than her. She didn't really think Wes was that type of man. He had always been honest with her, and she trusted him. But her ex-husband had not treated her as well. The scars left on her heart stirred her suspicion. She decided to be bold. Instead of wondering who she was, Mary would just go ask her.

Mary walked up to the door of the bar and pulled it open. There were only a few people inside, the mystery woman, and a bartender. She felt awkward as she walked up to the bar, where the woman sat. She couldn't remember a time when she'd walked into a bar alone. Nor had she frequented them often with someone else. It just wasn't part of her daily world. Now, as she settled at the bar, a stool away from the woman she had seen with Wes, she did her best to look as if she belonged there.

"A drink, ma'am?" The bartender set a napkin down in front of her.

"Just water, please." She hesitated. "With some lemon."

"Okay." He raised an eyebrow, then turned around to retrieve the water.

"Better leave a tip, they don't like it when you just order water." The woman beside her flashed her a grin.

Mary noticed that she was even prettier when

she smiled. But the smile didn't last. It faded, and she picked up her beer.

"Thanks for the advice." Mary smiled at the bartender as he set the water down in front of her. Then she turned her attention back to the woman beside her.

"I'm Mary."

"Lydia." She sighed, then took another swallow of her beer. "Lydia Pike."

The name struck her. It took her a second to realize why. Pike. It was Stuart's last name, too. Could this be his mother she sat beside?

"It's nice to meet you." Mary fiddled with her glass of water. "Are you from around here?"

"Look, I'm just here to drink a beer." She glanced over at Mary. "I'm having a rough day. I've just had some bad news."

"I'm sorry to hear that. If you want to talk about it, I've been told I'm a good listener." Mary took a sip of her water.

"People say that when you're boring." Lydia finished the last swig of her beer. "Another." She nodded to the bartender. "I'd prefer to sit in silence."

Mary nodded. She finished her water, then left a tip on the bar. As she walked towards the door she glanced back once. If Lydia Pike was Stuart's mother, she certainly didn't seem to be grieving over her son's death. She didn't shed a tear. Perhaps she was used to drowning her sorrows, rather than feeling them. No matter who she was, it didn't change the fact that Wes was hiding something.

~

*S*uzie arrived at the police station with the memory of Simon's grief on her mind. He seemed to be genuinely upset over the loss of his friend. When she stepped inside she found the station was busy. From what she could tell there were a lot of conversations about Stuart's death taking place. She noticed that Jason's office door was open, and spotted him seated at his desk. As she approached the door, he stood up, and walked towards her.

"Suzie, how are you doing?" He met her just outside of his office.

"Okay, so far. I just came from the hospital. I checked in on Simon. He's been released." She glanced towards the small television in the corner of the lobby. "It looks like he's just finishing up with the reporters."

"Of course." Jason sighed. "I tried to speak to

him earlier today, but didn't get much out of him. Alana was there." He narrowed his eyes as he saw her on the screen. "I felt like she didn't want me to talk to him much."

"She seems overprotective of him. It's not as if she's his agent." Suzie shrugged as she looked away from the television. "But he might be a good source of information. I was wondering if you'd had the chance to contact Stuart's mother yet. Simon had mentioned that she was here in town."

"I've tried to reach her, but the numbers I've found for her are all disconnected. I didn't realize she was in town, though." Jason frowned. "I'll have everyone keep a lookout for her. I've put a call in to Stuart's agent, I'm hoping that she will have more current information for his family."

"Good idea."

The door to the police station flew open, and a woman stepped inside with a flourish. Once Suzie looked in her direction, she couldn't look away. There was no question that she stood out amid the casual people of Garber. From head to toe she was dressed impeccably, and her hair drifted in perfect waves around her head. It was more than her beauty that held Suzie's attention, however. It was the way that she walked, how she carried herself, and the confidence that she seemed to exude.

"I need to speak to whoever is in charge here."

"Excuse me for a second." Jason frowned as he stepped away from Suzie. "Maybe I can help you?" He offered her his hand as he introduced himself.

"Perfect. I'm Jesinta Canda, Stuart's agent. Or former agent, I suppose." She shook his hand briefly. "I want to know what happened to Stuart, every detail, and what you are doing about it."

"I will share with you whatever information I can, and I'd appreciate it if you would do the same." As he led her into his office, he and Suzie exchanged a brief look.

As Suzie's phone rang, she pulled it out of her purse. Mary's name danced across the screen.

"Hi Mary."

"Suzie, I just had a brief conversation with Stuart's mother, Lydia Pike. At least, I think it's his mother." She took a breath. "Has Jason spoken to her, yet?"

"No, he hasn't been able to contact her. Where did you speak to her?" She grabbed a pen and pad of paper from a nearby desk. As she scribbled down the name of the bar, her thoughts swam. "Why were you at a bar?"

"It's a long story. I'm headed back to *Dune House*. Meet you there?"

"Yes, of course. I'll be there soon." Suzie hung up the phone then pulled the piece of paper off the pad. As she walked towards Jason's office, she could hear Jesinta's raised voice.

"It's been hours since he was killed and you're telling me that you still have no idea who did this?"

"Ma'am, it takes some time to sort these things out. We've collected evidence and are in the process of finding new information. What I need from you is some information about Stuart, his friends, his family, his enemies." Jason stood up behind his desk. "Can you help me with any of that?"

"He didn't have friends, other than Simon, and the hundreds of people that would show up at his parties. He didn't have family, other than his mother who only showed up when she could make money from it, and as for enemies, they are too numerous to list." She shook her head. "The point is he was killed here, and you need to focus on getting the job of finding out who did this, done."

"I'm doing my best, ma'am." Jason noticed Suzie through the door, and waved her inside.

"I've got some information about Stuart's mother." Suzie offered a brief nod to Jesinta before handing Jason the paper.

"Great, I'll send someone over there now." He pulled out his radio.

"She won't be any help." Jesinta rolled her eyes. "I'd be surprised if the old bag didn't kill him herself."

"Why would you say that?" Jason turned his attention back on her.

"Because, she's never done anything but push him. She never let him take a break. One time he injured his ankle, and she insisted he continue to train, even against doctor's orders. I don't know." Jesinta sighed and placed her hands on her hips. "I don't have any kids, but that doesn't seem right to me."

"No, it doesn't." Jason grabbed his keys from his desk. "Thanks for your time, Jesinta. I'll be in touch with any further questions, and I'll do my best to keep you up to date."

"I expect you to." She stepped aside as he headed out the door. When she fell into step behind him, Suzie followed after her.

"Jesinta?" Suzie touched her lightly on the arm to get her attention.

"Yes?" She turned swiftly towards her. "What is it?"

"I just wanted to say, I'm sorry for your loss. If there's anything you need while you're in Garber, please feel free to contact me." Suzie offered her a business card.

"Thanks." Jesinta took the card, glanced at it, then shrugged. "But I won't be here long. I'm a very busy person."

"I'm sure you are." Suzie managed a small smile, then walked towards the exit of the police station. Something about Jesinta left her unsettled. It seemed to her that Stuart had plenty of people in his life, but very few that actually cared about him.

CHAPTER 7

*W*hen Mary returned to *Dune House* she went straight to the yard and was greeted by an eager nuzzle from Pilot. She was comforted by his welcome, and leaned down to stroke his back. In the back of her mind she still wondered what Wes was doing alone with Lydia Pike. But she also knew that what happened to Stuart was more important than that. She needed to find the truth, and she knew that Suzie would be ready to help her with that as soon as she arrived.

Pilot followed her into *Dune House*. The quiet inside indicated that the guests who had chosen to remain there were not currently present. She'd barely seen them since that morning. She guessed they wanted to be as far from *Dune House* as possible.

"Let's get you some food, Pilot." Mary smiled and led the dog to his bowl. As she filled it, she heard the front door open and close.

"Mary, are you here?" Suzie called out from the entrance.

"In the kitchen, feeding Pilot." Mary straightened up and turned to greet her friend.

"How's Wes?" Suzie looked into Mary's eyes.

"He's okay." She cleared her throat. "Did you tell Jason about Lydia?"

"I did, and he's on his way to speak with her. While I was there, Stuart's agent, Jesinta arrived. According to her, Lydia wasn't much of a mother." Suzie frowned. "Jesinta didn't seem to be too broken up about Stuart's death, either. I think Simon might be the only one upset."

"I think that's the problem. I'm not sure that many people really knew Stuart. I think we need to find out what we can about him, if we want to help with the investigation." Mary added some water to Pilot's bowl, then walked over to her purse. "This is the most information I could get." She slapped a magazine down on the center of the dining room table. "I picked this up at the grocery store. It was right in the check-out aisle."

"Interesting." Suzie picked it up to find Stuart's face on the front page. "I knew that Stuart was popular, but I didn't know that he was this well-known."

"Apparently, he's been featured in an advertising campaign." Mary gazed at the cover as well. "But it doesn't seem like he has a very good reputation."

"You can't always trust what they write in these things, they just want to sell magazines." Suzie sat down and began to thumb through the glossy pages. When she reached the article about Stuart, her eyes widened at the pictures of his drunken nights, and female companions. "Wow, I guess pictures don't lie, though."

"He did seem to be a party animal." Mary sat down across from her. "But it's funny, when he stood up for Simon, it was like he was a different person. Confident, determined, and all of that in someone else's defense? It seems to me that someone who lives a carefree lifestyle wouldn't usually be so concerned about the feelings of others. Simon must have been special to him."

"Maybe that's not what he was concerned about." Suzie sat back in her chair as a possibility formed in her mind. "Maybe he was more concerned about losing the race. With Simon injured, I doubt the team had any chance of succeeding."

"You might be right. Since his public reputation already wasn't that stellar, he may have hoped that the race would help with that. He wouldn't have wanted to ruin a winning record." She sighed and leaned against the table. "Unfortunately, we can't know for sure what he was thinking. Maybe his social media will give us some clues?"

"There's plenty of it." Suzie picked up her phone and began to scroll through some of the pages that she already knew about. "It reads a bit like the magazine, I'm not sure how much weight to give it."

"If the only person that really knew Stuart was Simon, then we're going to have to find a way to talk to him." Mary frowned. "If he's willing."

"If we can get him away from Alana." Suzie narrowed her eyes. "She was all over him at the hospital. I'm not sure if it was just for the sake of the press, or some other reason. But it might be hard to get him alone if she's around him."

"Until then, I think the Parish team is a good place to start. Did Jason say he picked up Michael, yet?"

"No, not yet." Suzie sighed. "It's looking more

and more like he's hiding out intentionally. He could have even left the country by now."

"I know."

"Why were you in a bar, by the way?"

"It was next to the produce market and I found out Lydia was inside." Mary shrugged.

"Okay." Suzie nodded, but she sensed there was more to the story. She studied her friend for a moment. Her lips were pulled tight with worry. Her hands settled in a tight knot on her lap. "Mary, are you okay?"

"I'm fine." She nodded, and unfurled her hands. "I just have a lot on my mind. I think I'll check on the guest rooms again, and make sure they're tidy. Soon it'll be time to start dinner."

"I was planning on having a late dinner with Paul, is that okay? Would you like to join us?"

"Yes, that's fine. No, thanks. I think I want an early night." Mary smiled.

"Do you think anyone will come back for dinner?" Suzie stood up and followed Mary into the kitchen. "I can get things started."

"I'm not sure. Ali, Carter and Sam said they were eating out. But I don't know about the others, I haven't seen anyone since this morning." Mary started up the stairs. "If I hear anything I'll let you know."

Suzie watched her go. Her shoulders slumped as she climbed. It wasn't from pain, it was something different, Suzie could sense it. She was tempted to push the issue, but decided against it. She didn't want to pry. When Mary was ready to talk to her about it, she would be there to listen.

As Suzie focused on preparing dinner, she heard the front door open. When she turned, she found Charles in the entrance.

"Hi Charles." Suzie smiled at him. "Will you be joining us for dinner?"

"No, I can't. In fact, I'd like to leave Garber tonight. But the local police department has asked me not to." He crossed his arms. "It's pretty ridiculous, I feel like I'm being held hostage."

"I'm sorry that you feel that way." Suzie walked through the dining room to meet him. "But I hope you understand, this is all for the sake of finding out what happened to Stuart."

"What happened to Stuart is that he finally threatened the wrong person," Charles snapped. Then he held up his hands. "I'm sorry, I know it's wrong for me to talk that way, but I'm sick of hearing all of the sad songs people are singing over Stuart. He was a jerk, and everyone knows it."

His words hung heavily in the air before her. As she struggled for the right way to react, she could see the regret building in his eyes.

"Oh, was he that terrible?" Suzie met his eyes. "I didn't know him very well. Did he treat you badly?"

"If you call threatening to kill me and my family treating me badly, then yes." His gaze sharpened. "I officiated at the last race he was in, and he didn't like my ruling on an incident in the race. He told me if I didn't change it, he had ways of making me pay. Then he said he would start with my family, so I would have the chance to suffer." His eyes widened in horror. "Who talks like that? Over a race?"

"That's awful, Charles. I'm so sorry that he treated you that way." Her heart began to pound. She could see the anger was still fresh in Charles' eyes. Fresh enough for him to want to take revenge on Stuart? "I'm surprised that you wanted to work with him again after that happened."

"I didn't. I had no idea that he was going to be part of this race. Alana sprung that on me at the last minute. Now she thinks I'm going to meet her at the diner for dinner? She's nuts. She did this to all of us by allowing him to be a part of this race. He didn't belong in it, and she knew it." He waved his hand. "I'm sorry, I've got to go take something for this headache I have." As he moved past her she noticed that he had a strange scent. It reminded her of Paul right after he came back from a fishing trip, but just a little different. She sniffed him again, which caused him to look at her strangely. "Do you mind?"

"Sorry." Suzie blushed as she glanced away from him. "Have you been down by the docks?"

"I took a walk down there, yes." He hurried past her towards the stairs. "Hopefully, I will be checking out in the morning."

"Are you sure you wouldn't like some dinner?"

"I'll find something later." He disappeared up the stairs.

"Was that Charles?" Mary walked in from the kitchen.

"Yes, it was. He doesn't want to join us for dinner tonight." Suzie headed back towards the kitchen, uncertain if he was still near enough to hear her speak. She didn't want to repeat what he said until she knew that she and Mary were alone.

"Don't bother with dinner then, I just got a text from Jen that she and Shelly, and Andrew, are having dinner out." Mary sighed. "I guess no one really wants to be here."

"It's okay. It might be for the best." Suzie patted Mary's shoulder. "You know, Charles told me that Alana is planning to have dinner at the diner tonight. It might be a perfect time for us to try to talk to Simon. Maybe I could distract her at the diner, and you could pay Simon a visit? As far as I know he's staying at the *Garber Motel*. What do you think?"

"Perfect." Mary nodded. "But wouldn't you rather talk to him? You might get more out of him."

"I already tried at the hospital. I think it would be better if you give it a shot. You have a way of making everyone feel at ease." Suzie smiled at her.

"At ease, or bored?" Mary offered a dry laugh.

"At ease." Suzie met her eyes, and frowned. "Are you sure you're okay?"

"I'll be fine, don't worry." She gave her a light hug. "Let's do this before we miss our chance."

"Sure, let me just put these things away." Once the kitchen was cleaned up, Suzie met Mary on the porch. "You're sure you're up for this?"

"Absolutely. I just called and confirmed that Simon is staying there, and I got his room number. Just make sure you keep Alana talking for a while." Mary jingled the keys in her hand. "Here's to finding out the truth."

"Yes." Suzie jingled her own keys, then followed Mary to the parking lot. As they went in two different directions, she couldn't shake the feeling that there was a lot more on Mary's mind than just Stuart's murder.

When Suzie pulled into the parking lot of the diner she found it was pretty packed. She guessed that most people were dining out in an attempt to get the latest gossip about Stuart's murder. She hoped that one of those cars belonged to Alana. She was about to step out of the car, when her cell phone rang. She picked it up when she saw Jason's name on the screen.

"Hi, what's up?"

"I just wanted to let you know that we picked up Michael about an hour ago."

"Oh, thank goodness. Did he confess?" Suzie held her breath, hoping that maybe all of this was over.

"No, the opposite actually. He has an alibi. I'll fill you in on the details later, but I wanted to share the update. I really just wanted to let you know he's been found. I know you were worried."

"Thanks Jason." Suzie sighed as she hung up the phone. With Michael eliminated as a suspect, she knew that Jason would have a lot more to sort through. It made her desire to speak to Alana, even more urgent.

As Suzie entered the diner, she found with relief, that Alana was seated alone at one of the tables.

"Hi Alana." Suzie paused beside her table and looked at her with a gentle smile. "Sorry to bother you."

"It's no bother." She smiled in return. "My dinner date stood me up. Would you like to join me?"

"Sure, thanks." Suzie sat down across from her, but kept her eyes on the woman. Dressed in a navy blue suit, with matching navy blue earrings and a navy blue teardrop necklace, it was clear that she paid close attention to how she looked. Despite how neatly she was dressed, her expression was nervous. She chewed on her lip as she looked at Suzie.

"I'm sorry that all of this happened here, Suzie. I know it has to be hard on all of you." Alana glanced around the diner at the other customers, then looked back at her. "I'm sure a quiet town like this isn't used to such a scandal."

"No, it's not." Suzie spared a smile for the waitress, Pam, as she poured her a cup of coffee. Then she looked back at Alana. "I'm sorry about the race."

"Honestly, I pushed for it to go on. I don't know why they need to cancel it. I know that might sound cruel, but so many people invested in this day. The athletes give so much of themselves, their time, their bodies, and to have it all canceled is hard." Alana flicked her gaze in the direction of the other customers in the diner. "And to have the police indicate that they need to stay longer is crazy. Don't they know these people need to go home to their families? I have no idea what they were thinking. But what can you expect? I'm sure the people in charge aren't exactly well-trained or experienced."

"I wouldn't say that." Suzie bristled as the urge to defend Jason rocketed through her. "I can understand your frustration, but Stuart was murdered. An investigation has to occur. It would be quite difficult for the police to track everyone down if they returned to their hometowns."

"Everyone knows it was Michael." Alana flicked her hair back over her shoulder, again, and rolled her eyes. "I honestly don't know why they haven't arrested him already."

"There is a very good reason." Suzie narrowed her eyes as anger continued to flood through her. Alana's dismissive attitude towards Garber, and the police that kept it safe, had her on edge. "The police here don't arrest innocent people."

"Innocent?" A forceful laugh erupted from between her lips, followed by a short snort. "Michael had every reason to want to kill Stuart. What makes him so innocent?"

"His alibi." Suzie knew that Jason might not appreciate her spreading that information around, but Alana had a know-it-all attitude that had her last nerve plucked. "He couldn't have killed Stuart."

CHAPTER 8

$\mathcal{M}$ary headed in the direction of the *Garber Motel*. It was a small place that usually had very few guests, but with the race in town it had become more popular. She drove past the cars parked in front of each motel room, until she found number eight. The parking spot was empty. She guessed that Simon had been using taxis, as most of the out-of-town visitors had been. She parked in the empty spot, then walked up to the door. After a quick knock, she heard the rustle of movement beyond the door. A moment later, the door swung open.

"Hi? Can I help you?" Simon narrowed his eyes as he studied her. She noticed the sling on his arm, and the rumpled state of his clothing.

"Hi Simon. I'm Mary, do you remember me?" She offered him a warm smile.

"Oh Mary." He nodded as he returned her smile. "I remember. From the beach, and when I crashed my bike." He looked past her, into the parking lot, then back at her. "What are you doing here?"

"I just wanted to check on you. I know when my son broke his arm, he had a hard time doing a lot of things. I was a little worried that you being here all alone, you might not have the help that you need." She peered past him into the motel room. She could see scattered piles of his possessions. "Do you have anyone to help you?"

"No, not exactly." He took a step back. "You can come in if you'd like. Sorry about the mess." He blushed as she walked past him into the motel room. "I wasn't expecting a guest."

"Oh, don't worry about that." Mary settled in one of the chairs at the small table near the window. "Have you eaten? I can go pick up some dinner for you if you'd like."

"I just had some pizza." He pointed out an empty pizza box on the small kitchen counter. "Thanks though." He sat in the chair across from her. "I really appreciate you checking in on me, but I'm okay."

"You don't have to put on a brave face for me." She smiled. "I know that your arm hurts, and I'm sure your heart does, too. You've lost a friend after all."

"Yes, I have." Simon closed his eyes. "I wish I could turn back time. I wish I could have been there to protect him. I warned him not to pick so many fights, but he never listened."

"Did he pick any fights while he was here?" She leaned forward some.

"He had some kind of argument with a fisherman. Then he went after Charles, because Charles demanded that he not be allowed to participate in the race. I even heard him screaming at his agent on the phone. He fired her, can you believe that?" He rolled his eyes. "His temper, it never quit."

"He fired his agent? I didn't know that." Mary made a mental note of it. At this point it seemed that Stuart had far more enemies than he did allies. "Why would he do that?"

"He had landed this big account, a magazine spread, and a sponsorship. But after his last party, the sponsor dropped him. He insisted it was Jesinta's fault because she couldn't convince the sponsor to take him back." Simon licked his lips, then sighed. "The way he talked to her, it was insane. I told him, no one deserves to be spoken to like that. But he wouldn't listen."

"You know, I've heard that he had a terrible attitude. You seem like such a nice young man. Why did you stick around when everyone else walked away from him?" Mary studied his expression as it shifted from annoyed to something else, something darker.

"I guess I thought if I was just nice enough to him, eventually it would rub off on him. But it didn't, no matter what I did, he was still a jerk." Simon shook his head. "I hate to say that, but it's the truth."

"But he was kind to you?" She met his eyes. "Or did he treat you just as badly?"

"No, he was kind. Generous. He would buy me anything I wanted, take me anywhere I wanted to go. I guess he was just grateful to have a friend that didn't abandon him." His cheeks flushed. "I tried to be there for him. I really did. He was so alone underneath it all. He was so lonely."

"I imagine he was. Even his mother wasn't there for him." Mary clucked her tongue. "That is a terrible way to grow up."

"They were poor, you know? As soon as she found out that Stuart had athletic talent, she started pushing him. Really hard. He never did anything but train when he was a kid. I guess that's why he liked to party so hard once she didn't have power over him anymore. I thought maybe she was in town to try to reconcile with him, but when I told him she was here, he just got angry. He didn't want to have anything to do with meeting her. I thought maybe if he could mend that relationship he would start to be a little less angry. But her being around only made him more angry." He ran his hands back through his hair. "I should have tried harder to protect him."

"Hey, that wasn't your job." Mary squeezed his free hand. "You were a great friend to him. You did everything you could to protect him, even when he wouldn't listen to your advice. I know this is hard, but it's not your fault, Simon."

"Maybe not." Simon pulled his hand from hers. "But it sure feels like it is. Thanks for stopping by, Mary, but I really should try to get some rest."

"Of course." She stood up and gazed at him with some concern. "Simon, don't beat yourself up about this. Stuart wouldn't want you to."

"I guess." He shrugged, then walked her to the door.

As Mary stepped out, she turned back to let him know he could contact her if he needed anything, but he closed the door before she could. Her heart ached for the young man who had lost his friend, and for the young man who had lost his life. Maybe Stuart wasn't exactly a good person, but he'd never had the chance to be. He'd been abandoned by the person who was supposed to love him the most. Was it possible that she was cruel enough to kill her own child? Mary couldn't believe that it was.

~

*S*uzie noticed the pure shock in Alana's expression in reaction to her revelation about Michael's alibi. To be honest, she found it just as shocking, and even hard to believe. She hoped that Jason would fill her in when she had a chance to speak with him, but she still wondered if he might have gotten something wrong. It seemed Michael had the strongest motive, and the best opportunity to kill Stuart.

"What alibi?" Alana's eyes locked to hers. "I haven't heard anything about that."

"It's police business. Honestly, I shouldn't have said anything at all about it. I imagine that anyone who didn't have an alibi at the time of the murder is now a suspect." She studied Alana for a moment longer. "Speaking of which, where were you at the time of Stuart's death?"

"Excuse me?" Alana stared at her with clear disdain. "You couldn't possibly think that I had anything to do with this."

"I'm not saying that you did. I'm just curious about where you are staying. I know that the *Garber Motel* is full and —"

"I rented a house. Several of the contestants are staying there, as well as their coaches." She pursed her lips. "I was there the whole time after I left the memorial."

"I see. And Stuart? Where was he staying? Was he staying there?"

"No, he was staying at the motel in Garber. But he wasn't there last night, apparently. One of the other contestants told me that he didn't come back at all after the event dinner."

"Really?"

"Yes, but that didn't surprise me." She shrugged. "And it wasn't my concern."

"What about his coach? Wasn't his coach concerned?"

"Actually, Stuart was the coach of his team. He refused to accept anyone else. He said he had the most experience and could coach his team the best."

She picked up her glass and took a drink. "He always got what he wanted. Like I told the police already, his high demands and spoiled behavior won him more enemies than friends."

"Did you tell them about Stuart's absence last night?" Suzie searched the woman's eyes for any hint of emotion.

"No. It isn't my place to share that kind of information." She locked her eyes to Suzie's, not the least bit intimidated.

"The police have a hard job to do. The more information you can give them, the better the chance of this murder being solved. That seems pretty important to me."

"You're right, it is." Alana's eyes widened. "I honestly thought they had this thing wrapped up. I didn't realize that Michael was cleared." She picked up her fork, then put it down again. "Now we have no idea what happened to Stuart. This is very upsetting."

"Yes, it is." Suzie met her eyes, though the moment she did Alana glanced away. "That's why it's so important for everyone to cooperate. Is there anything you can tell me about Stuart? My friend Mary and I are having a hard time understanding how this could happen. We've tried to get to know him a little better by looking him up, but everything out there seems pretty negative."

"I know what you mean." Alana took a deep breath, and as she exhaled her shoulders drooped. "Honestly, I didn't even want him to be part of this race. I thought his presence would bring the wrong kind of attention. However, his agent insisted that he be allowed to be part of it. I should have put my foot down." Her eyes fluttered shut, and she sighed. "Maybe he would still be here if I did."

"It's not your fault, Alana." Suzie placed her hand over Alana's and gave it a light squeeze. "There are a million ways he might have avoided this, but the only one who is responsible for his death is the person who killed him."

"You're right." Alana offered a brief smile, then pulled her hand away to pick up her fork again. "I suppose it was inevitable, with his lifestyle. But I always thought it would be a drunken crash, or something of that nature, not murder."

"So, the stories about him are true? He was always partying and getting into trouble?" Suzie furrowed a brow as she noted the way that Alana's eyes filled with tears.

"Yes, as far as I know. He didn't seem to value his life very much. Or maybe he just considered his pleasure to be more important. Whatever the thought process, I couldn't understand how he could be so athletic while abusing his body to such a degree. Honestly, it was hard to watch."

"You mentioned that Stuart made some enemies. Was Charles one of them?" Suzie sat back in her chair and recalled the details that Charles had shared with her.

"Charles? Well, yes." Alana frowned and pushed her food around on her plate. "He is a nice enough man. He's worked with me on these races for a few years now. He's very fair. Most of the contestants really like him, because they trust him. But not Stuart of course." She rolled her eyes.

"Charles mentioned something about Stuart threatening him over a decision he made during a race." She tipped her head a little closer to Alana's and lowered her voice. "Do you know anything about that?"

"Yes, that was a tough race. He claimed that Stuart had sabotaged another contestant, intention-ally collided with him. Stuart insisted that he had to prove it. But Charles pointed out that it was his call, he could decide on his own, and he decided to disqualify Stuart from that leg of the race. It infuri-ated Stuart. He said some terrible things to

Charles." Alana closed her eyes for a moment. "I suppose none of that matters now. Charles will never have to deal with him again." She gestured to the waitress. "Can I get the check, please?" She looked back across the table at Suzie. "I believe I've lost my appetite."

Suzie sensed a coldness in her voice that left her unsettled. Was she angry at all the questions, or angry because Michael had an alibi? She couldn't tell which, but of one thing she was certain, Alana was angry.

CHAPTER 9

*M*ary sat in her SUV for a few minutes as she processed the information Simon had given her. Lydia was not a great person, that much was clear. That made her wonder even more what Wes was doing meeting with her. Did he know that she was Stuart's mother? Was it part of an investigation? She wanted to believe that, but the memory of Lydia's good looks left her feeling more than a little insecure. No, she wasn't the ugliest woman alive, but time and neglect had left her with blemishes, and extra weight, that Lydia didn't seem to have. Of course, Wes could have his pick of women. He was handsome, a successful detective, and one of the kindest men she knew, once she got past his gruff exterior. It had taken her months to believe that he was actually interested in her. Now she wondered if she had believed too quickly.

As Mary sat in the SUV she saw a motel room door open. She looked towards it and her mouth dropped open as she noticed Wes in the doorway with Lydia. She hugged him briefly then he turned away as she stayed inside and closed the door. He walked towards the street. Mary watched as he carried on walking down it. Her heart raced. Wes must have parked down the street. What was he doing in Lydia's room? Why did she hug him?

When Mary's phone buzzed she jumped. She saw it was a text from Suzie, she read it over. Michael had been found. He had an alibi. Another text said she was running late and was going to go straight to meet Paul for dinner. A third text suggested that she speak with Charles again about his connection to Stuart. Mary responded that she would, then started the SUV. What was going on between Wes and Lydia couldn't be her focus at the moment, what was important, was solving Stuart's murder.

When Mary arrived at *Dune House* she noticed someone on the front porch. She couldn't tell who it was until she got closer, then she recognized

Charles. She smiled at him as she climbed the steps.

"Charles, how are you?"

"Starving, honestly." He frowned. "I don't feel comfortable going out for dinner. There are some crazy rumors flying around about me."

"Why don't I make you something? The fridge is stocked." She reached for the door, but he stepped up quickly to open it for her. She shot him a brief smile of gratitude, then stepped inside. When he followed after her, a small chill crept along her spine. What if he was the killer? Was she alone in the house with him?

Pilot barked from the yard in that moment, as if to insist that she wasn't. She laughed as she went to let him in the house. He bounded up to her and she greeted him with a few pets and scratched behind his ear.

"I guess you're hungry, too, huh buddy?" Mary glanced over her shoulder at Charles. "Do you like dogs?"

"Some of them." He shrugged. "He seems pretty friendly."

"He is. He can get a little over-excited at times, but he's getting better about that. Aren't you, pal?" Mary pet him again, and laughed as he licked her hand. "How does soup and a sandwich sound, Charles? Ham and cheese? Or would you rather something else?"

"No, that sounds just fine, thanks." He settled at the dining room table, which was only a few feet away from the entrance of the kitchen.

"I'm sorry to hear about the rumors." Mary washed her hands, then began to prepare his food. "Do you want to talk about them?"

"The thing is, Stuart and I had a pretty intense run-in at another race. Since then he made no secret of the fact that he despises me." He sighed and sat back in his chair. "Yes, I was angry. He threatened me and my family. He tried to have me fired, and when he found out that I would be an official at this race, he tried to insist that I be removed. If it wasn't for Alana, I would have been out of a job. Luckily, she stood her ground and I was allowed to stay."

"Wow, it sounds like he really had an ax to grind with you." Mary warmed some vegetable soup for him, then brought his sandwich and soup to the table. "What would you like to drink?"

"Lemonade, if you have it, please." He rubbed his forehead. "I should have something stronger, but at this point I think that would make the rumors even worse. I can't wait to go home and forget that all of this happened. Of course, I'm still going home without a paycheck."

"Alana isn't paying you for your time here?" Mary walked back to the kitchen to retrieve his lemonade. As she turned around she heard him groan.

"No, of course not. She said that since the race had been canceled, she no longer owed any of the officials or athletes any form of payment. She even stopped covering the rooms for everyone. That's why so many people are so eager to leave." He shrugged as he took the glass of lemonade. "No offense, Mary, you have a beautiful place here, but I don't have the money to shell out for multiple nights while this investigation goes on. I'm going to have to check out tomorrow morning, and find somewhere cheaper until we're allowed to go home. Honestly, I'd just head out now, but I know that will only make me more of a suspect."

"Oh Charles, how stressful for you." Mary sat down across from him. "Stay tomorrow night, free of charge. Hopefully, by tomorrow everything will be figured out."

"Really?" Charles stared across the table at her. "You would do that for me?"

"Sure, I would. It's so unfair that you are being

accused of such a terrible thing, and in my opinion Alana should still be paying you for your time. If a free night here can help ease some of that stress, then I think you should absolutely have it." Mary raised an eyebrow. "Unless there's some other reason that you don't want to stay?"

"No, there's not." He smiled at her. "The hospitality has been fantastic. I did have a little trouble sleeping, but I always do."

"Was your bed comfortable? I can get you some extra pillows if you need them." She studied him with some concern.

"The bed was fine. Sometimes I just can't sleep. A walk by the water usually helps." He lowered his eyes quickly. "But enough about that. This sandwich is delicious, thanks."

"You're welcome." She smiled, but she noticed that he hadn't taken a bite. "Have you taken a walk by the water at night here, yet? The way the moon shines across the water is spectacular."

"Oh yes, I did. It was quite beautiful." Charles took a bite of his sandwich.

"So, you have seen it then? It must have been last night when you did." Mary watched him as he chewed very slowly. When he finally finished, he shook his head.

"No, I was asleep last night. All night."

"Then when? Because it was cloudy and even rained a bit the first night you were here. No moon at all." She locked her eyes to his and recognized the fear that surfaced in them as he realized his mistake. "Are you sure it wasn't last night?"

"Uh, no it wasn't. I guess maybe it wasn't here." He set his sandwich back down on his plate.

"Is it okay?" She smiled. "Do you need mustard?"

"No, it's fine, thanks." He managed a smile.

"Well, I think I'll let you eat in peace. I need to feed Pilot before he decides to get into the food himself." Mary stood up from the table, but kept her gaze on him. "You know, Charles, people do like to spread rumors. I find the best way to combat rumors, is to tell the truth. The truth can't be twisted."

"Thanks for the advice." Charles looked down at his soup.

As Mary took Pilot's dish outside and filled it with food, she was certain that Charles had lied to her. He hadn't slept all night. In fact, she was certain that he had gone for a walk by the water. Which meant he could easily have had something to do with Stuart's death. Had they run into each other somewhere out there? Had an argument led to something tragic?

~

Suzie had a relaxing dinner with Paul, talking about everything except for the murder, even though it was on her mind. When she returned to *Dune House* there was no sign of Mary or Pilot, so she presumed they must already be asleep. She got changed and then went straight to bed. After tossing and turning for a few minutes, thinking about what she needed to do the next day to help find Stuart's killer, she fell asleep.

The following morning Suzie woke up later than usual and found no sign of Mary, Pilot or any of the guests. She had a quick shower, grabbed a muffin and texted Mary asking if she was okay to take care of breakfast, as she wanted to go straight to see Jason. Mary replied that was fine, and she would catch up with her later.

Suzie drove to the police station running through everything she wanted to ask Jason in her mind. She presumed he would be there early. She entered the police station and immediately sensed tension in the air. It was so thick, that she almost decided to leave. She guessed that with the revelation that Michael had an alibi, the entire mood of the investigation had shifted. Garber had a fairly low crime rate, and Jason had likely directed all of his resources to solving Stuart's murder. She made her way to the door of his office and after a light knock stepped inside.

"Hi Jason, how are things going?" Suzie pushed a stack of paperwork slightly to the side so that she could perch on the edge of his desk. There was nowhere else to sit, as all of the chairs in the room were occupied by boxes or other stacks of paperwork.

"I'm drowning." He sighed as he glanced up from the open file on his desk, which was splayed across a few more stacks of paperwork. "There are so many people to interview, so many people to do background checks on, and so many people calling to say how angry they are that they have to stay a day longer." He flipped the file closed, then pressed his fingertips against his forehead. "If only Michael had been a viable suspect, maybe this would be a bit simpler."

"So, you're sure about that?" Suzie met his eyes as he lowered his hands. "He isn't a suspect at all anymore? I thought since they had clear animosity towards each other, the fact that he was staying at *Dune House*, and the sheet that Stuart was found wrapped up in was from *Dune House*, that he was the main suspect. You're sure his alibi is strong?"

"You thought right, he was the main suspect. I was pretty confident that we knew exactly who killed Stuart. But Michael's alibi is airtight." Jason stood up from his desk, careful not to knock over any stacks. He walked to his office door, opened it up, and called out into the station, which was teeming with activity. "I need those background checks now, not one hour from now, and certainly not tomorrow. Let's get this done!" He stepped back into the office and closed the door with a heavy sigh. "I hate riding them like that, I know they're doing the best they can. We're all just under a lot of pressure." Jason smiled as he met her eyes. "Thanks Suzie, for stopping by. It reminds me there's still an outside world, beyond this mess." He gestured to the piles of paperwork. "I've even extended the suspect search to anyone in Parish or Garber at the time of the murder that has any history of violent crime. Once the media gets hold of this being a murder, they are going to fry this entire police department if we don't get this solved."

"I'm glad I could help at least in that way. Jason,

I know it can seem overwhelming, but you will figure this out." Suzie smiled in return, then watched as he returned to his desk. "Out of curiosity, what was Michael's alibi?"

"Ah, well, he doesn't want too many people to know about it, but it's going to get out eventually. Apparently, he is on a very strict diet for training, but he binge eats when he's nervous." Jason opened the file on his desk back up again. "He was in Parish at a twenty-four-hour diner, eating several slices of pie. I spoke to the manager on duty, and the waiter who served him. They both confirmed that he was there. He even gave them tickets to the race. I'd say that's a pretty solid alibi. He didn't even know what happened until we finally took him into custody. It's still possible he was involved in some way I suppose, but he certainly isn't the one who killed Stuart, or put his body into the water. So now the question is, who did? And unfortunately, I have quite a few possibilities."

"If there's anything I can do to help you with that, just let me know." She studied the strain in his expression with some concern.

"Actually, there is one thing that you could do." Jason looked up at her. "We did catch something interesting while looking over the surveillance videos from the dock. It's something I don't want to believe, but it has to be investigated, and it's our best lead at the moment."

"Did you see who put Stuart's body in the water?" Suzie held her breath, knowing that it wasn't likely, but still hoping.

"No, unfortunately that area of the dock is not covered by cameras. However, we did catch Stuart having an argument on the day before the murder, with one of the fishermen, a man named Carl." He tapped the file in front of him. "He doesn't have a criminal history to speak of, but that doesn't exclude him. The problem is he refuses to come in to speak to me. I would prefer if he came in for questioning voluntarily. I tried to talk to him, but he refused to answer the door. I know that Paul knows most of the fishermen around here. I thought maybe you could talk to him? If he knows Carl, maybe he could encourage him to come in and talk with me. What do you think? Would he do that?"

"I can ask him." Suzie nodded as she started towards the door. "I'm sure he will help in any way that he can."

"Great. I appreciate it, Suzie. Make sure he knows, I just want to talk to Carl." Jason locked eyes with Suzie. "It's just a first step. I know dealing with the authorities isn't Paul's favorite thing, either. I hope he can trust me on this."

"Okay, I'll make sure he knows. He does trust you."

"Oh, I almost forgot, did you hear about the memorial tonight?"

"No." Suzie shook her head.

"Garber is hosting a memorial for Stuart at the auditorium. Something to honor his memory."

"That's nice, I'll be there." Suzie smiled. "Jason, don't forget to take care of yourself. You still need to eat and sleep." She swept her gaze over his pale features and bloodshot eyes. "You're not going to solve anything if you can't function."

"I will. I'll take a break." Jason nodded and offered a light wave of his hand, before he looked back at the file.

As Suzie stepped out of his office and into the chaos of the station she felt a sense of urgency to help find the truth. Not only for Jason's sake, or Stuart's, but for everyone that would now be considered a suspect.

CHAPTER 10

*S*uzie drove towards the docks with her mind spinning. Carl? She didn't think she had ever met him, but the idea that the killer could have been someone local made her feel terrible. Could Stuart have come all the way to Garber only to be murdered by a fisherman with a short temper? She knew that Paul would probably be able to tell her more about it when she asked him, but would he want to? It made her uneasy to put him in the position of having to speak against someone he might consider a friend. But in her past as an investigative journalist she'd had to put people in worse positions to get a story. The question was, would Carl be willing to talk? She parked, then walked towards Paul's boat. She spotted him before she could reach it, as he stood with a group of three men near the main office. The other men dispersed as she approached.

"Hi Paul." Suzie frowned as she watched his friends scatter. "Is everything okay? I didn't mean to scare them off."

"It's pretty tense out here right now." Paul rubbed his hand along the back of his neck. "Everyone's riled up over Jason closing the docks, because of the investigation. We aren't allowed to move our boats, yet. Everyone wants answers."

"I know." Suzie gently placed her hand on his chest and looked into his eyes. "He is trying his best to solve this, but he might need some help."

"I know he is." Paul leaned against a wooden pole and gazed at her. "But I'm not sure too many people will be talkative."

"I can imagine. Knowing that Stuart's body was put into the water right here has to be pretty unsettling." She skimmed the boats that lined the dock, then looked back to him. "Does anyone seem particularly upset?"

"I'm sure some are pretty upset about it, but that's not the source of the tension. At least not most of it." He looked towards the boat closest to them, scanned it, then returned his attention to her.

"People are upset because they can't move their boats from the docks at the moment and there is still a ban on fishing near the docks, even though the triathlon has been canceled. They want to get back to work, since they already lost time and money from the last couple of days. I have to say, I understand their frustration."

"Aren't they the least bit concerned about finding Stuart's killer?" Suzie pursed her lips, then began to pace. "If they start fishing again, critical evidence could be lost, or contaminated."

"What evidence?" He stood up from the pole, his eyes following her back and forth motions. "It seems to me that the only thing the police could find in the water, is water. Stuart's not there anymore."

"Well for one, it's possible that a fisherman was involved in this." Suzie paused, and looked straight at him. "As you just said, people here were frustrated about the ban on fishing. Maybe someone wanted to get the race canceled, or at the very least, some pay back."

"What?" His eyes widened as he looked back into hers. "You can't be serious."

"I am, absolutely serious. In fact, when Jason checked the surveillance footage on the docks he saw Stuart get into an argument with one of the fishermen here. Carl. Obviously, there was no audio, so he couldn't get an idea of what they argued about, but when Jason tried to speak to Carl about it, he wouldn't say a word." She studied him in an attempt to predict his reaction to her next question. "How well do you know Carl?"

"Carl?" He crossed his arms as his expression darkened. "I know him real well. We've been working on these docks together for a long time. He keeps to himself, but he's a good man. There's no way he was involved in any of this. Are you sure you've got the right person?"

"That's who was on the surveillance video." Suzie placed her hand on his forearm and gave it a gentle stroke. "I'm just asking. I'm not accusing."

"Well, that's just impossible." Paul frowned as he unfolded his arms, then took her hand. "He's got two kids at home to support. Why would he ever do something that would cause him to lose everything?"

"I don't know. I can't answer that. But did he ever mention to you that he was upset with Stuart?" Suzie lowered her voice as another fisherman walked past. Once he had continued on, she leaned closer to Paul. "Anything he said to you could help clear him."

"Or make things worse." He narrowed his eyes as a forceful breath escaped his lips. "Listen Suzie, I know you're going to report back to Jason whatever I tell you. Carl is my friend, and I know him, he couldn't have done this."

"If it's the truth, then you shouldn't have to worry about it. Don't you want Stuart's murder solved?" Her fingertips grazed his cheek as his jaw rippled with tension. "That's all I'm trying to help do here, Paul. You know I would never want to do anything to upset you. But something has to give the police a direction to go in, and if you know something, then yes, it's important for Jason to know about it. Paul, you know he doesn't want to put anyone in prison that doesn't belong there."

"Suzie, I can't stand by and watch my friend be railroaded for something that I know he didn't do." Paul released her hand and took a step to the side. "You have to understand. Fishermen look out for each other. It's about loyalty. Can't you trust me when I tell you that he had nothing to do with this?"

"I do trust you, Paul, you know that." Suzie stared into his eyes. "And, I do understand your loyalty, but this isn't about money, or politics, or even friendship. This is about a man who lost his life, right here in Garber." She slid her hands into her pockets and allowed him his distance. "If Carl wasn't involved, then help me to prove it. Give me something that will encourage Jason to look in a new direction."

"I don't know anything that will do that." Paul raised an eyebrow as he stared into her eyes. "Let's just drop it."

"Wait, but you do know something, don't you?" Suzie took his hand again, though he tried to pull it away. "Paul, you don't have to hide anything from me."

"I do if I think you're going to run straight to Jason with it. Suzie, I want Stuart's killer caught, you know I do. But Carl is innocent, and I don't want to send the wrong man to prison because of something I said. You can understand that, can't you?"

"I understand that." Suzie frowned. "What I don't understand is you thinking that you can't trust me. You just asked me to trust you, and I do. If you say Carl wasn't involved, then I believe it. But if you can't trust me, or Jason, enough to know that any information you give me would only be used to find the killer, then that is a problem."

"I do trust you, Suzie. I do." Paul cupped her cheeks and gazed at her. "But I don't want to get my friend into trouble when I know he would never have hurt Stuart. I couldn't live with myself if I get Carl into trouble, maybe even arrested, for something he didn't do."

"But if Carl knows something that can help solve the crime, can you live with yourself if you don't share that?" She studied him. "I don't think you can."

As her heart slammed against her chest she realized that getting angry with Paul wasn't going to do anything to benefit the investigation. The truth was, she understood his concern. She had seen investigations go the wrong way in the past. There was never a guarantee that an innocent man would be protected from wrongful imprisonment. But she needed to know what he knew, no matter what it was.

"Suzie." Paul sighed. "This is impossible."

"You're right. I'm not being fair to you. You can tell me what you know about Carl. It can be just between us." She searched his eyes. "I won't say a word to Jason."

"Can it?" He held her gaze. "I don't want to put you in a position where you have to lie to Jason."

"Trust me, Paul." Suzie frowned. "Isn't that what we're supposed to do?"

"All right." Paul nodded as he gazed at her. Then he took a deep breath, and began to speak in a low tone. "Carl and Stuart had a run-in the day before the charity race. He was on his boat, and Stuart zipped up on a jet ski. You know, they're not allowed near the docks. Carl hollered at him to get out of the area, and Stuart yelled back that he could be wherever he wanted to be." Paul glanced over his shoulder as a few fishermen passed. When he turned back, his cheeks were flushed. "It almost came to blows. If they had both been on land, I think it would have. I went over to intervene, but before I could Stuart took off. Carl was pretty angry about it. He had good reason to be. But not reason enough to kill someone. That's why I didn't want to tell you. It will only make Carl look guiltier. But it was just an argument, nothing more. Carl can be hotheaded sometimes, especially if someone is breaking the rules, but he's a good person, Suzie. I wouldn't want to protect him if I didn't believe that."

"I believe you, Paul." Her heart pounded as she realized that now she'd put herself in a terrible position. "An argument that almost came to blows." Suzie could understand Carl's anger. There were signs posted all around the area warning jet skiers to stay out. It wasn't safe with the larger boats going in and out because of the wakes they created, and the likelihood that the jet ski would be overlooked as a boat backed out or pulled in. There was no reason for Stuart to be there, other than to thumb the rules.

"See, that's how it will be taken. But Carl wouldn't kill him. Maybe he would have punched him, but he wouldn't have killed him. He's just a regular guy trying to make a living. Suzie, if he gets accused of something like this, he'll never get back on his feet. It doesn't matter if he's innocent, his reputation in a small town like this will suffer." He shook his head. "If I hadn't seen it, there would be nothing to tell."

"But you did see it." She bit into her bottom lip as she considered her options.

"And now you know." He stared at her. "Are you really going to be able to keep this between us?"

"Yes I am." Suzie met his eyes. "Because you're going to convince Carl to speak to Jason."

"What?" He frowned. "I never agreed to that."

"Listen Paul, the longer Carl resists having an interview, the more suspicious he will look. It's up to him what he tells Jason, but the only way the heat is going to turn down is if he starts cooperating. I made you a promise, and I will keep it, but you have to make an effort to get Carl to clear his own name.

Do you think you can do that?" Suzie raised an eyebrow.

"I can try." Paul sighed, then looked out over the water. When he looked back at her he nodded. "I'll do my best, Suzie. But I can't guarantee you that he will talk to him."

"I understand. That's all I'm asking, is for you to try." Suzie forced down the urge to text Jason right away with the information Paul had given. The truth was it wasn't much different from what Jason already knew. Except it was evidence that Carl and Stuart had engaged in more than one argument. "Paul, thank you for telling me. Thank you for trusting me." She cupped his cheek, then kissed him lightly on the lips. "I hope that you know you always can."

"I do." He returned the kiss, then drew her close for another, more passionate embrace.

For a few seconds, Suzie forgot all about Stuart, and the investigation. She lost herself in the moment with Paul. A moment later a whistle from one of the other fishermen, jerked her back to reality.

"Keep quiet!" Paul shouted at the fisherman. "Sorry, Suzie." He frowned as he looked back at her. "Some of these guys just never grow up."

"It's all right." Suzie smiled. "I have to get going."

"Where are you headed now?" Paul called out to her as she headed back towards the parking lot.

"I'm meeting Mary at home for lunch. Do you want to join us?" She paused and looked back at him.

"No, I've got some work I need to get done, but I'll be at the memorial tonight." He met her eyes.

"See you there." Suzie smiled then walked to her car. As she settled inside, she could see *Dune House* up on the hill. She wondered what Mary might have discovered. She hoped that it was something that would steer the investigation away from Carl. She did trust Paul, but his years of friendship with Carl might make his opinion biased. What if he was wrong?

CHAPTER 11

*M*ary looked up from the paper she had been jotting notes on, as Suzie stepped through the door.

"Hey there." She smiled at her. "How's Jason?"

"Overwhelmed." Suzie sat down at the table beside Mary. "Is anyone else here?"

"No, Charles is out, and the rest of the guests have checked out for cheaper accommodation I suppose, since according to Charles, Alana is no longer covering their stay here." Mary frowned. "I hope you don't mind, but I told Charles he could stay just one more night for free."

"I don't mind at all. I have some news for you." Suzie shared the information about Michael and Carl. "Honestly, I want to believe that Carl is innocent, but it's hard to argue video, and two incidents of arguments. He certainly had the opportunity. I just hope that he is willing to speak with Jason, maybe he will find a way to clear Carl's name."

"Carl may seem suspicious, but I think Lydia is far worse." Mary winced as she shared her conversation with Simon, then moved on to her suspicions about Charles. "I think he's lying about where he was the night of the murder. I think he might have seen something, or worse been involved in something. But my suspicion is still on Lydia."

"As much as we may want to jump on the idea that she did this, we don't have any proof of that." Suzie shook her head, then sighed. "If we're going to prove it, then we're going to need a lot more to go on."

"You're right. My instinct is to dislike her, but that doesn't make her a killer. It is concerning that she could potentially make more money from his death than she could from his fading career."

"What do you mean?" Suzie's eyes widened.

"I did some research this morning, and there were some articles about her taking out a large life insurance policy on Stuart when he was still a teen. It caused a bit of a scandal. She pointed out that athletes put themselves at risk all the time and that it only made sense to have an insurance policy on him." Mary cringed. "Still, the public didn't take it well."

"I wouldn't either." Suzie narrowed her eyes. "That certainly is interesting. So, Lydia was estranged from her son, likely not receiving much income from his sponsorship or modeling anymore. She could see his career was potentially coming to an end, and maybe she thought it was the right time to just be rid of him." She stroked Pilot's fur a few times. "What a terrible thing to consider."

"Terrible, but possible." Mary pursed her lips. "Or maybe I'm just being more suspicious than I should be." She sighed as she looked down at the table.

"Mary, it's time you told me what's really going on here." Suzie leaned close to her, then wrapped her arm around her shoulders. "I know whatever it is has you very upset. You need to tell me the truth, maybe I can help you."

"There's no way you can help me." Mary sighed and closed her eyes. "Suzie, it's Wes."

"Wes?" Suzie frowned as she studied her friend. "What about him?"

"He's hiding things from me." She shifted in her chair, opened her eyes, and looked directly at her.

"He's been meeting with Lydia, but he didn't tell me about it. Why would he be meeting with her?"

"Mary, I'm sure that he has a reason. Wes is a good guy." She curled her hand around Mary's. "Have you asked him about it?"

"Not exactly. I've given him the chance to tell me the truth, but he just avoided it. Suzie, I think he's in a relationship with her." Mary lowered her voice to hide the waver in it. "It's not exactly like we've said we're exclusive, I guess these days relationships are far different."

"That's a big leap to make, Mary. Are you sure about it? Have you seen proof?" Suzie sat back in her chair. Could Wes be capable of something like this?

"Not exactly. I've seen them very close, and he hugged her. I don't know, Suzie, I just wish he had told me the truth. I know I'm not the most exciting person for him to be dating. I would understand if he had an interest in someone else. But to lie to me about it? I thought he cared about me more than that." Mary winced. "I guess that was just me being foolish."

"Listen Mary, if he is doing this, then he's not worth your time. But I'll be honest, I wouldn't expect something like this from Wes. I think you need to give him a chance to explain." Suzie stood up from the table. "Maybe tonight, at the memorial? The people of Garber want to have something to honor Stuart's memory. I'm sure Wes will be there. Pull him aside, ask him what's really going on." She gave Mary's shoulder a light pat. "I'm hoping he's going to have a good explanation for this. But if he doesn't, you need to remember, it's not because of you. You're an amazing person, and he is lucky to be with you. If he doesn't see that, then he's an idiot." She gave her a light hug. "It's okay to feel jealous, and uncertain. It's normal. Right now, you don't know what's going on with Wes. I still think you should talk to him, though, just ask him. Tell him what you know, don't let him avoid it."

"But what if he's trying to protect her?" She shuddered at the thought. "What if he knows what she did?"

"No." Suzie shook her head firmly. "No way. I can't believe that about Wes, and neither can you, not if you're honest with yourself."

"You're right." Mary's shoulders drooped. "I'm just letting my imagination run away."

"It's okay, Mary. You care about Wes, he's important to you, and he's keeping secrets from you. That's never easy to accept." Suzie stood up from the table. "Talk to him, Mary. Give him the chance to tell you the truth. I'm going to see if I can find out what Charles was up to on the night of the murder. If he was out near the water, someone on the docks might have seen him. Not that they will necessarily talk to me about it, but it's worth a try."

"Let me know what you find out." Mary stood up from the table as well. "I'll do my best to talk to Wes, you're right. I need to at least give him the chance to explain."

~

As Suzie walked towards the docks, she noticed a police car in the parking lot. Then she spotted Jason a few steps away from it. He seemed to be in a heated conversation with a man who stood in front of him. Suzie approached slowly, knowing that she might not be welcome to interfere. When Jason glanced over his shoulder, she knew that he had sensed her presence.

"Suzie." He locked eyes with her. "I was just about to call you. Could you join us, please?"

"Sure." She held his gaze in an attempt to figure out what was happening.

"This is Carl." Jason tipped his head towards

the man in front of him. "He asked for you to be present while I talk with him."

"He did?" She spared a small smile at Carl, who she couldn't recall ever meeting before.

"I had nothing to do with this. But that doesn't matter, does it?" Carl looked from Suzie to Jason. "I'm on camera having an argument with the dead guy. So that makes me the killer."

"Maybe not." Jason placed his hands on his hips. "But it sure doesn't look good that you refused to come in and cooperate. That tells me that you have something to hide."

"I didn't come in, because I knew that all of this would get pinned on me. I don't have any money for a lawyer." Carl sighed as tension filled his expression. "I don't want to go to prison, okay?"

"I'm not in the business of putting innocent people behind bars, Carl." Jason took a step towards him. "I would think that you know that already."

"Maybe Jason, maybe in most cases. But this isn't most cases. This is practically a celebrity, just a kid, I know how things go when money is involved. It doesn't matter if I'm innocent, people want someone to lock up, so they can move on, and I'm the perfect fit." He looked over at Suzie. "If it wasn't for Paul, I wouldn't be here right now. He told me that I could trust you, and I'm trusting him."

"You can trust me." Suzie looked into his eyes. "No one is here to accuse you of murder, Carl. You're here because you may have been one of the last people to see Stuart alive. We were hoping that maybe you saw something, or someone, that might point us in the direction of the real killer."

"But it wouldn't hurt to know where you were between three and five yesterday morning." Jason cleared his throat and shot a brief look of warning at Suzie.

"I was at home, in bed, with my wife." He frowned and clenched his hands at his sides. "But I know that's not a good enough alibi. I don't know why you think I'd be one of the last ones to see him alive, I didn't even see him that night."

"Because you were on your boat at two-thirty." Jason nodded.

"Well, yes, I was," he stammered. "I stayed late to do some clean up on the inside, since I couldn't do any fishing off the docks. But I left at two-thirty. I never saw Stuart."

"How about anyone else?" Jason locked his eyes to Carl's. "Anyone at all. Maybe someone you barely noticed as you walked past? Or voices? Someone arguing?"

"No, no one." He shook his head and crossed his arms. Then he took a slow breath. "Well actually, I guess I did see someone, but not on the dock. In the parking lot."

"Okay, who was it?" Jason shifted closer to him. "Someone you recognized?"

"I don't like to get into anyone's business." He tipped his head to the side. "You know, what people choose to do, that's not my concern."

"Carl." Suzie clenched her teeth, then did her best to speak in a calm tone. "This is important. Stuart lost his life, and we need to know why. If there's anything you can tell us, it might help."

"I don't see how." He took a deep breath, then shrugged. "It was just somebody making a bet. Probably on the race, but I don't know for sure."

"Who was it?" Jason's voice became sharper, edged with urgency. "Who did you see?"

"Hal, you know Hal, right?" He shivered. "I don't want to get on the wrong side of that guy. I've seen what he does to people."

"Hal Jenkins, yes, I know him." Jason's eyes narrowed. "We've been trying to get him on something that could stick for a long time, but nobody is willing to testify against him."

"Me either." Carl took a step back and held up his hands. "I have kids, you know."

"All right, just calm down. All I need to know is who he was talking to." Jason pinned Carl with an intense stare as he took a step towards him. "Tell me that, and you're free to go."

"I didn't see." Carl looked down at the wooden slats beneath his feet. "I just hurried past. All I know is it was Hal, I heard his voice."

"Who was he talking to, Carl?" Jason's tone grew more stern.

"I didn't see!" Carl snapped in return.

"Okay, okay." Suzie stepped between the two men, and looked into Carl's eyes. "What did Hal say? You said you heard his voice. What did you hear him say?"

"He said, nobody gets a free pass, what's due is due." Carl swallowed hard. "That's what I heard. That's why I left." His voice cracked, then he looked up at Suzie. "You must think I'm some kind of coward. I left because I knew things were about to get messy, and I just wanted to get home to my wife."

"It's okay, Carl." Suzie's throat tightened with

emotion as she saw the fear in the man's eyes. "There was nothing you could have done."

"But maybe there was." Carl glanced past her at Jason. "I swear, I didn't know he was going to kill the kid. If I had known that, maybe I would have done something. Maybe I would have called the cops." He clasped his hands together in front of him. "Maybe."

"You saw Stuart there, with Hal?" Jason's expression remained grim.

"No, I didn't see who it was, I swear. I just figured it was someone who lost on a bet. I didn't think too much about it, to be honest. I just knew I didn't want to get in the middle of it."

"Carl, you had your family to think about." Suzie met his eyes. "You made the right decision to keep yourself safe. And you made the right decision by coming forward to talk with Jason."

"What you just told me, could make the difference in solving this case, Carl." Jason met his eyes.

"So, I'm free to go?" He looked between the two of them.

"For now." Jason nodded. "I am not going to take you in at this time. I can't justify it just because you had a disagreement with Stuart and you were present on your boat before the murder. If I can speak to Hal and have him verify that he saw you leaving the dock, that will make things even better. I do expect if I call you, that you'll answer." He raised an eyebrow. "Can I count on that?"

"Yes, you can." Carl nodded, then turned and hurried off.

"Do you believe him?" Suzie glanced over at Jason.

"I want to." He rubbed his hand along his chin. "But first, I need to speak to Hal."

CHAPTER 12

*M*ary stared at her phone. She'd sent Wes a text twenty minutes ago, and had yet to hear back from him. Wes almost always texted back within just a few minutes. Despite trying to convince herself that she was overreacting, she was worried. Was he with Lydia? She imagined all kinds of reasons that he would avoid her text, and none of them were good. She was just about to put the phone into her purse to leave for the memorial, when it buzzed in her hand. Wes had responded.

Yes, I'll be at the memorial. I'll see you there.

She studied the text and wondered if there was more to his reason for going. Would Lydia be there, too? Was that why he didn't offer to drive with her, because he was escorting Lydia?

"All right, that's enough, Mary." She sighed and tucked her phone into her purse. She did her best to push her concerns about Wes out of her mind, and focus instead on the memorial. There was a good chance that Stuart's killer would be at the memorial, and she didn't want to be distracted from spotting any clues. As she headed out the door, she found Suzie had just mounted the front porch steps.

"Suzie, I was just heading out to the memorial, I can wait though if you want to go together."

"Yes, that would be good. Jason has a new lead." Suzie smiled as she approached the door. Mary trailed behind her, curious.

"Other than Carl?"

"Yes, I honestly don't think Carl had anything to do with it, although he hasn't been cleared yet. It turns out that he did see someone on the dock, two people, but he could only identify one of them. Hal." Suzie led Mary to her room, and grabbed a dress to change into.

"Hal? Isn't he some kind of bookie?" Mary frowned.

"Yes, he is. Apparently, he was shaking down someone for money at the same time that Carl left his boat around two-thirty. Which means that Hal and one other person were likely on the dock at the time of Stuart's death. Give me just a second." She stepped into her bathroom, changed, then joined Mary in the bedroom again.

"So, either Hal was meeting with Stuart, or at the very least, he might have seen Stuart." Mary's eyes widened. "That's a great lead."

"Yes, it's possible that Hal was even meeting with Stuart's killer. Jason is trying to hunt him down now." Suzie ran a brush through her hair, then touched up her make-up, before she followed Mary down the hall. "The only problem is that Hal is not likely to be talkative. He's known to be shady, and I doubt he's going to want to share much information with Jason. Do you think Stuart had a bet with Hal that he couldn't cover? Maybe that's why he got so upset about Simon being injured. Maybe he had bet on his team to win the race, and when Simon was injured, he tried to get out of the bet, but Hal killed him instead."

"It's possible." Mary nodded. "But why would he kill him? It's not like he could recover money from a dead man, and with Stuart's wealth and fame he would have eventually paid his debt."

"Maybe, or maybe not. Stuart liked to party, right? He had recently lost a contract with a magazine, and he'd fired his agent. Maybe he wasn't doing so well financially, and he didn't want to pay the debt. He and Hal could have argued, maybe Stuart even attacked him, and Hal killed him. Anything is possible at this point. Until Jason finds Hal, it's the best lead we have." She shrugged as she walked towards the door.

"Other than Lydia." Mary frowned. "She could still be behind all of this."

"Yes, she could be. Did you get a chance to talk to Wes?" Suzie pushed open the door and held it open for Mary.

"No, he said he would see me at the memorial. Hopefully, I can get a few minutes alone with him there." Mary lowered her voice some. "If Lydia isn't with him that is."

"It's going to be okay, Mary." Suzie wrapped her arm around her friend's shoulders. "Either you will find out a reasonable explanation for Wes' behavior, or I will teach him a lesson he will never forget."

"Aw." Mary flashed her a brief smile. "That does make me feel a little better."

"I thought it might." She gave her shoulder a pat, then opened the car door. "Let's hope that something is revealed tonight, or Jason is able to track down Hal. Stuart will finally get his justice."

"I hope so." Mary nodded as she settled into the car.

The parking lot of the auditorium where the memorial was being held, was already packed by the time Suzie parked in one of the few remaining empty spots. Several news vans were parked near the entrance of the building.

"I think the news that Stuart was murdered is out." Suzie frowned as she stepped out of the car. "Things are going to get very tense, very quickly."

"I wonder if Jason is ready for this?" Mary matched her pace as they approached the auditorium.

"I hope so. He's a great detective, but handling the media is an entirely different beast. Especially when dealing with a high-profile victim." She held open the door for Mary, then followed her inside. "I guess we're about to find out."

Mary recognized several people gathered together in tight knots. Some were athletes, others were locals. But many more were people she didn't recognize. She guessed that word had spread to some of Stuart's associates in other cities and states.

"For someone who had more enemies than friends, he certainly has quite the turn-out for his memorial service," Mary murmured softly to Suzie as they lingered away from the others.

"Yes, he certainly does. Everyone wants a piece of the media splash. It'll be news for a few days, then they will move on to some other scandal." Suzie narrowed her eyes. "Stuart will only be remembered by the people who cared about him."

"Like Simon." Mary tipped her head towards the man who stood with a group of athletes. His arm was still in a sling, and the look of exhaustion on his face made her wonder if he was still in quite a bit of pain.

"Yes, we should get a few minutes with him when we can. I'd like to ask him if he knew anything about Stuart being involved with Hal." Suzie's gaze swept over the crowd. "Have you seen Paul?"

Mary froze as she caught sight of a very familiar face. Wes stood in the shadows cast by an overhang not far from the large group of people, but far enough not to be noticed. Beside him, was Lydia.

"Mary, did you hear me?" Suzie glanced over at her after her question was left unanswered. She followed her friend's gaze to the pair hidden in the shadows. "Is that Wes?"

"And Lydia." Mary nodded, her voice tight.

"Are you going to go over there?" Suzie gave her shoulder a slight nudge with her own. "We need to know what Lydia might be saying to him."

"Okay." Mary took a deep breath. "Yes, I'm going over there." She walked towards them. "Hi Wes." Mary paused about a foot away from the two. In the shadows of the overhang she couldn't quite read their expressions, but she was certain that she had interrupted something.

"Mary." Wes offered her a brief smile, then glanced back at Lydia. "This is my girlfriend Mary."

"We've met." Lydia raised an eyebrow. "Though I had no idea you two were together."

"I guess we're even then, because I have no idea how you two know each other." Mary did her best to sound pleasant, but an edge crept into her voice that she wished wasn't there.

"We're old friends." Lydia leaned into Wes some and lowered her voice. "We went to high school together."

"You did?" Mary's eyes widened. "But I thought you've always lived in Parish, Wes?"

"I have." He glanced over his shoulder at the gathering crowd, then looked back at Mary. "So did Lydia. Listen Mary, can you give us just a few

147

minutes? I need to speak with Lydia about something."

"Okay." Mary stared at him for a long moment as she realized he was trying to get rid of her. But why? Whatever the reason, she didn't trust the fact that he wanted to be alone with Lydia. However, she wasn't going to make a scene at a memorial. She nodded to them both, then headed towards Suzie, who stood quite close to Charles and Alana.

"So?" Suzie shifted close to her as soon as Mary walked up. "What did he say?"

"He asked to be alone with Lydia." Mary frowned, then looked back over at the two. "I'm trying not to think too much of it, but apparently they might have been high school sweethearts at one point. Lydia is originally from Parish."

"She is?" Suzie's eyes widened. "Well, that surprises me. Maybe that's how she knew her way around here so well to track her son down."

"Maybe." Mary tipped her head towards Charles and Alana who appeared to be shifting from pleasant conversation into an argument. "What's going on between those two?"

"I'm not sure. Charles walked up to her, I was going to listen in." Suzie turned her attention back to the pair.

"You need to back off, Charles, or I will get the authorities involved." Alana glared at him as she took a step back from the finger that Charles thrust in her direction.

"That's not such a bad idea. Maybe they can help me to find out where my paycheck is?" He took another step towards her. "You can't play games with people like this, Alana. Do you understand me?"

"I haven't canceled the race completely, yet. I'm hoping to just be able to postpone it until next weekend. If you would just be patient, then we could get all of this figured out. But instead, you have to rush things." Alana shook her head and crossed her arms. "Watch that temper of yours, Charles, this wouldn't be the first time that it's gotten you into trouble."

"Oh, you'd like that wouldn't you?" He stared at her, his eyes wide, and his mouth half-open. "You'd like everyone here to believe that I have some kind of uncontrollable temper. That way, I look more guilty. But nothing you can say or do will make me guilty of a crime I didn't commit, Alana. You keep saying you might still have the race, fine, then pay me for the time I've spent here, and if you want me to stay for the next race then I will. But I need the money that you owe me, now."

"I don't owe you any money. You haven't done anything, yet! There was no race!" She threw her hands up in the air and rolled her eyes. "And really? At Stuart's memorial? Should you even be here?"

"Don't push it, Alana. You know I had nothing to do with what happened to Stuart. But I don't see you coming to my defense. You agreed to pay me for travel, for room and board, and for the time I've spent here. That is all I'm asking for, what you agreed to pay me. I have bills to pay, Alana." He frowned.

"Don't you think I do, too?" She raised an eyebrow. "It's not as if I made any money from this race."

"That's not my problem. You should have the money to pay the staff before you even begin to plan a race." Charles took a slight step back as he studied her. "That's it isn't it? You don't have the money."

"Of course, I have the money. I just can't be rash in dispersing it. I'd like things to settle down before I start handing it out. Forgive me if I'd like to grieve over the loss of my friend before I handle business—"

"Your friend?" Charles emitted a sharp laugh. "That's rich."

150

"Charles." Alana snapped at him. "Have you been drinking?"

"I want my money, Alana." He stared hard at her, then turned and walked away.

"Is everything okay, Alana?" Suzie moved a little closer to her.

"Fine." She waved her hand, then turned and walked away.

"Interesting." Mary crossed her arms. "I wonder if Alana and her business were having some financial trouble even before all of this happened."

"It's possible." Suzie narrowed her eyes as she stared after the woman. "Whatever might have been happening, we both certainly know that she didn't consider Stuart a friend."

"True." Mary nodded as she turned to see Wes walking towards her.

CHAPTER 13

"*M*ary?" Wes caught her hand as he walked up to her. "Can I steal you away for a few minutes?" He met her eyes, his tone serious.

"Sure." She glanced over at Suzie. "You'll be okay?"

"Yes." Suzie looked past her friend and locked eyes with Wes. She didn't say a word, but the sharpness of her gaze made Wes raise an eyebrow.

"Over here." Mary steered Wes towards a quieter spot.

"Is she okay?" Wes glanced back in Suzie's direction. "She seems upset."

"She's fine." Mary turned to face him, her own

eyes hard as they settled on his. "Are you finally going to tell me what this is all about?"

"Mary." He tightened his grasp on her hand. "Why are you upset with me? Why is Suzie glaring at me?"

"Why are you sneaking around with an old friend from high school?" Her voice wavered some as she spoke, but she continued to hold his gaze.

"Oh no, Mary." He sighed and tugged her a little closer to him. "Is that what you think, that I'm sneaking around with her? That there's something between us?"

"What am I supposed to think?" Mary looked past him, in the direction of Lydia, who Simon had now gravitated towards. "You haven't told me anything."

"Because I can't, Mary. Some things I simply can't tell you. But I expect that you are able to trust me enough to know that I would never do anything to hurt you." He touched the curve of her cheek. "Don't you?"

"I want to." She sighed as she met his eyes again. "But she might have killed her own son, Wes. Why would you ever want to be around her?"

"You think that she murdered Stuart?" He

shook his head as a frown creased his brow. "There's no way she would do that. She loved her son."

"You must know a different woman than the one I know. The woman I know used her son, and neglected him." She searched his eyes. "How can you call that love?"

"Mary. You're a spectacular mother. I didn't have to meet your children to know that. I can see it in your eyes, and the way you are with people, and the way you were with your children, how caring you are. But not every mother is that way. Yes, Lydia was hard on Stuart, but that doesn't mean that she didn't love him. I can't tell you why I've been meeting with Lydia, but I can tell you that she is heartbroken over the loss of her son." He pulled her a little farther away from the crowd. "The reason I've been meeting with her has to do with an investigation, that has nothing to do with Stuart's murder. At least it didn't, but now I'm not so sure."

"Can't you tell me anything about it?" She lowered her voice to a whisper. "I would never want you to risk the integrity of an investigation, but I don't understand how you can be so certain that she didn't do this. She had motive, and she had opportunity."

"All I can tell you is that she was helping me

with an investigation. She wasn't here to hurt Stuart. I reached out to her because I knew she had a connection with the person I was investigating. I promised to keep her safe. I hope that nothing I did put Stuart in danger." He shook his head, then ran a hand across his forehead. "I'm not sure exactly what happened, but I am trying to get to the bottom of it." He looked into her eyes. "But none of this has anything to do with us, Mary. I would never do anything to hurt you. I hope that you know that."

"I do." Mary frowned as she returned his gaze. "It is just hard to understand why you were sneaking around."

"Try not to worry about it. When this is all over, I will be able to tell you everything. Can you just hang on for me that long?" Wes looked into her eyes.

"Yes, I can. Of course." Mary managed a smile, then watched him walk back towards Lydia. She had wrapped her arms around Simon in a tight embrace. Mary crept a little closer so that she could overhear their conversation.

"I'm sorry you never had the chance to talk with him." Simon pulled back and frowned as he studied Lydia. "I'm sure it would have at least given you some closure to have seen him again."

"I'm sorry, too." Lydia nodded slowly. "I had really hoped that we could reconnect. Simon, I know I wasn't the best mother. I don't pretend I was. But I did what I thought was best for him."

"I guess." Simon cleared his throat. "There's no point rehashing the past now. Stuart is at peace, at least that much we can be grateful for."

"Perhaps." Lydia looked past him, straight at Mary. "Or maybe he will never know peace until his killer is found."

"It won't be long, Lydia." Wes touched her shoulder as he returned to her side. "I've told you, this is going to be solved soon enough."

"I hope so." She narrowed her eyes as she looked away from Mary, to Wes. "Thanks for your support, Wes. I can always count on you." She wrapped her arms around him.

Mary looked away. She couldn't help but believe that the last comment was meant for her to hear. Was she being paranoid again?

When Mary turned back in Suzie's direction, she noticed that she had started a conversation with Alana. As she walked over, she heard some of their discussion.

"I'm sorry he was behaving that way." Suzie

frowned. "It's really not the right time or place for it."

"No, it's not." Alana crossed her arms.

"But did I hear you right? You're still thinking of having the race?" She raised an eyebrow as she met the woman's eyes. "Do you think that's wise?"

"I think it might be the best option for everyone involved. Of course, I would want to give it a few days, and let things settle down." Alana glanced in the direction of the room where the memorial would be held. "Quite a turn out."

"Yes. It is." Suzie gestured for Mary to join her. "I just want you to know that if you need anything, Mary and I are here to help."

"Thank you, I do appreciate that. However, I won't be staying. I plan to leave tonight after the memorial. The best way for me to get the race to continue is to get back home and iron some things out. Of course, we'll have to find a new location. It would just be insensitive to host the race in the same town that Stuart died."

"Was murdered, you mean?" Suzie searched the woman's intent expression. She seemed more concerned about the race than she was about Stuart's murder.

"Yes, of course." Alana stared back at Suzie as a hint of annoyance entered her voice.

"Aren't you the least bit concerned that whoever did this to Stuart could do it again? What if it's one of the athletes that signed up for the race?" Suzie clutched her purse. "I would be so nervous that someone else would become a target."

"Hopefully, by then the killer will be behind bars." Alana narrowed her eyes. "As far as I'm concerned the killer is most likely a resident of Garber. No offense, but apparently this isn't the safest town."

"It usually is." Suzie shrugged as she held the woman's attention with a steady gaze. "However, someone decided to commit a terrible crime here. Have you told Jason that you will be leaving tonight?"

"No, I haven't. I wasn't sure that I needed to. I'm not exactly a suspect." Alana laughed, then turned towards the door that led into the memorial. "I'd better get a seat, I'd hate to be stuck at the back."

"Cold." Mary sighed as she stared after the woman. "Something is off about her."

"I'd say so. Interesting that she thinks she's not a suspect. I wonder why? As far as I know, she doesn't have the greatest alibi. She said she was at the house she is staying at, in her room." Suzie turned towards the door as well, but something caught her attention out of the corner of her eye. "Mary!" She caught her hand. "It's Michael." She pointed to a man who lingered near the entrance. He looked nervous as he peered inside.

"Oh wow, he probably shouldn't be here." Mary took a step forward, but before she could intervene, Simon lunged towards the door.

"What are you doing here?" Simon pushed Michael back outside with his free arm. "I can't believe you'd have the nerve to show your face! After what you did to me. After what you did to Stuart!" The rage in his voice drew the attention of several people around him.

Suzie sensed the mounting tension. She had a fairly good idea of what would happen once Simon got Michael outside, and it wasn't pretty.

"We'd better get out there!" Suzie gasped as she grabbed Mary's hand.

As they headed out through the door, Mary cast a look back inside in search of Wes, but there was no sign of him, or Lydia.

"Simon, please calm down. I just wanted to pay

my respects." Michael held his hands up in the air as he backed away from Simon.

"Pay your respects? You sick bastard!" Simon lunged towards him again, but not before Suzie managed to catch him by the arm.

"Simon! Calm down! What is this all about?" Suzie stepped in front of him.

"What do you think? He doesn't belong here. He was no friend of Stuart's. He knows what he did!" He glared at Suzie, but didn't attempt to move her aside.

"I thought you believe what happened to you was an accident?" Mary stepped up on the other side of Simon. "Did something change your mind?"

"Alana told me the truth. She told me that Michael did it on purpose to try to throw the race." He shook his head as he stared at Michael. "You're sick! You could have killed me!"

"Alana told you that?" Michael stumbled back. "She's lying. I didn't do it on purpose. You can't prove that."

"Can you?" Jason walked towards the four of them from the parking lot. "Simon, would you like to make a formal complaint against Michael?"

"No, no I don't want any trouble." Simon looked edgily in Jason's direction. "But he shouldn't be here. If he was willing to injure me, then what would stop him from killing Stuart? His mother shouldn't have to sit in the same room with the man who might have killed her son." He looked towards Suzie and Mary. "You can understand that, can't you?"

"Yes, of course." Mary nodded. "But you can't be sure that Michael had anything to do with Stuart's murder. He's been cleared by the police, he has an alibi."

"She's right, he does." Jason hooked his thumbs into his belt and looked between the two men. "And I'm afraid that Michael has the right to be here, just like anyone else."

"It's all right, I'll go." Michael took a step back, his hands raised again. "I don't want to cause any trouble. I just wanted a chance to say goodbye. I admired Stuart. I really did."

"Why don't you and I take a ride and talk about it?" Jason gestured to the police car in the middle of the parking lot.

"Why? Are you going to arrest me?" Michael shied back from him.

"No Michael. You have an alibi, remember? I just want to talk with you. Maybe you know more than you think." Jason gestured again to the car.

"All right." Michael nodded, then glanced over at Simon, Suzie, and Mary. "I'm sorry to have disturbed all of you." He turned and followed Jason to the car.

"Absolute garbage." Simon sneered at the retreating man's back. "He should be arrested."

"But you said you didn't want to press charges?" Mary stared at him. "Why is that?"

"It doesn't matter. I just don't want to. I need to get back inside." Simon spun on his heel and headed back through the doors.

"I guess we'd better get in there, too." Mary gave Suzie's arm a gentle tug. "We don't want to miss it."

"You're right." Suzie stared after Jason and Michael for another moment, then followed Mary inside. Suzie glanced back over her shoulder once and scanned the parking lot for any sign of Paul. She was sure he'd said that he would be there, but his car was not in the parking lot. She pulled out her phone to text him, but as she was swept up in the crowd that entered the room she realized it wouldn't be appropriate.

Throughout the memorial several people spoke. Most were famous people that had come in from out of town for the memorial. Suzie didn't recognize all of them, but a handful were athletes she had seen on television before. Each spoke glowingly about Stuart, which indicated to Suzie that they didn't actually know Stuart very well or were putting on an act. With plenty of cameras and reporters, she guessed that this was an opportunity for them to get some media attention. Notably missing from the crowd, was Stuart's agent, as well as Lydia.

"Do you know where Lydia went?" Suzie leaned close to Mary as she whispered the question.

"I'm not sure." Mary shook her head. "I didn't see her leave. But Wes is over there." She tipped her head towards the stage. "He's alone."

"Interesting." Suzie frowned as she wondered what could pull a mother away from her son's memorial. Clearly, Lydia wasn't your average mother, but it still seemed incredibly cold.

CHAPTER 14

*a*s the memorial ended, Suzie and Mary started for the door. Suzie stopped suddenly at the sight of Paul in the doorway.

"Hey sweetheart, I'm sorry I wasn't here earlier." He hugged her. "I guess I missed everything."

"Yes, you did, what happened?" Suzie met his eyes and guided him away from the crowd.

"I just got caught up and didn't realize what time it was." He frowned. "Can you forgive me?"

"Sure, but I was looking forward to having some time with you." She smiled at the warmth in his eyes.

"Can we meet at *Dune House* in about an hour? I want to pay my respects, and then I have one more errand to run." He kissed her cheek. "Is that okay?"

"Yes, that's fine. I'll see you there." She squeezed his hand.

As she left the auditorium, she caught sight of Mary as she said goodbye to Wes. She stepped up beside her friend.

"Is everything smoothed out now?"

"I think so. He has no idea where Lydia went either." She shook her head. "She just disappeared."

"I think we should take a walk through town. It might clear our heads a bit. Are you up for it?" Suzie raised an eyebrow.

"Sure, that sounds good." Mary took a deep breath of the night air. "Wes is convinced that Lydia had nothing to do with Stuart's death, but I can't say the same."

"It does seem pretty suspicious that she took off like that. Alana's speech about him was quite nice though." She led the way towards the center of town.

"Suzie! Isn't that Hal?" Mary grabbed her hand and tugged her off to the side. "Look, he just went down that alley!"

"Let's catch up to him!" Suzie ran towards Hal, with Mary following her. Before Mary could catch up, Suzie had Hal trapped at the end of the alley.

"Hal!" Suzie stared straight at him. "Don't you know that Jason has been looking for you?"

"In general, I try to avoid the police." Hal glared at her.

"Hal, you need to be straight with me." Suzie looked into his eyes as he shifted from one foot to the other. "I know that you were meeting with Stuart, not long before he died. What was it about?"

"I never saw him." Hal crossed his arms. "You can't prove anything. If you could, I would be behind bars."

"That can be arranged." Suzie lifted an eyebrow as she stared at him. "One call to the police, and you can discuss this with them inside of an interrogation room."

"All right, take it easy." He gazed at her with a curled upper lip. "You want to play the tough guy, huh? I don't want any trouble. I'd rather be talking to the two of you than anyone with a badge."

"All right then, talk." Suzie moved closer to him. "Why were you meeting with Stuart that morning?"

"I told you, I didn't meet with Stuart. I was there with someone yes, but it wasn't Stuart." Hal cleared his throat. "I can't tell you who it was. All right? It's not your business. It has nothing to do with Stuart's murder."

"You have to tell us." Mary stepped between Suzie and Hal. "Every detail of that morning matters. Who you were talking to, matters."

"Back off!" He scowled at both of them. "I don't have to tell you anything!"

"Fine, then I'm calling the police!" Suzie pulled out her phone.

Hal lunged forward and knocked the phone from her hand. As it crashed to the ground, he started to run, but tripped over her phone in the process. It sent him sprawling across the pavement.

Suzie snatched her phone from the ground, then straightened up.

"Hal, you shouldn't have done that." She began dialing Jason's number.

"They'll never catch me!" Hal quickly stood up, shoved between them and bolted down the alley. Suzie started to chase after him, but Mary grabbed her arm.

"Wait, Suzie. We might have something better."

"What? He's getting away!" Suzie frowned as she waited for Jason to pick up. "Now I won't be able to tell Jason where he is."

"Maybe not, but we have this!" Mary held up Hal's phone. "He must have dropped it when he tripped. It could have a record of who he was meeting with."

"He said it wasn't Stuart, do you think he was telling the truth?" Suzie paused as Jason finally answered the phone. Once she filled him in on what they'd found and Hal's most recent location, a siren instantly fired up in the distance. "He's on his way." She hung up the phone.

"Honestly, I think he might be telling the truth. I think Hal was meeting with someone else, and that person might have been the one to kill Stuart."

"If it is, hopefully this phone will give us some clue. I'm not sure that Jason can just look through it, legally. Maybe we should have a quick look." Suzie took the phone from Mary. "It's still open. Let me see if I can find his call history." She skimmed through the phone, then nodded. "I've got it, but there are no names, just phone numbers."

"What about texts?" Mary peered at the phone as well.

"They're just numbers, too, but there are a few from around the time of the murder." Suzie began to read them off. "I'll be there soon, we can work this out, you need to calm down. Then he returns the text, and says, you owe me that money, there's nothing else to work out, you don't get any special favors, Princess."

"Princess?" Mary's eyes widened. "I don't think too many people call men princess, do you? That means whoever he was texting was likely a woman."

"I think you're right. But who?" Suzie looked over the remainder of the texts. "It's just a bunch of threats from Hal. They agree to meet around the time that Carl saw someone on the dock with Hal. He must have seen whoever was texting Hal."

"Not whoever, a woman." Mary nodded slowly. "This eliminates a few people as suspects. Michael, obviously, and Charles. It also verifies what Carl said, he really did see Hal on the docks that night, at the time he claimed."

"Who does that leave us?" Suzie frowned. "Lydia? Jen, the coach from Parish?"

"What about his agent?" Mary raised an eyebrow. "Just because she claims to have come into town after Stuart's death, doesn't mean that she isn't lying."

"True. And there's Alana." Suzie pursed her lips.

"Alana?" Mary tipped her head from side to side. "Yes, she's a possibility, though I'm not sure what her motive would be."

"Let's try the number and see who answers?"

Suzie shrugged as she dialed the number. After a few seconds she frowned and hung up. "It's disconnected."

"There's Jason." Mary turned towards his car as he pulled up to the alley.

"What do you have for me?" He walked towards them, his expression anxious. "I've got cars out hunting Hal down."

"It's Hal's phone." Suzie offered it to him. "It's still open. I found a text from someone we think is a woman, discussing meeting with him at the docks about the time that Carl claimed to see him. I tried the number, but it's disconnected."

"You know that just because you found the phone, doesn't mean that you can look through it?"

"We just wanted to see if we could find out some information, so we could return it to him." Suzie smiled sweetly.

"Right." Jason rolled his eyes. "Let me see what I can find. There was a call from Stuart's phone to Hal's, but it's not the last call he made. The last call he made was from his phone to his mother's phone. It was about twenty minutes before the time of his death." He shook his head as he looked up at Suzie. "It's so hard for me to believe that a mother could do this to her own son, but what if she did? What if she killed him to cause the race to be canceled? Maybe she placed a bet on him to win, a large one, but with Simon out of the race there was no chance his team would win. She stood to lose a lot of money. Maybe she got desperate, maybe she thought it was the only way out." He gripped the phone tightly in his hand. "If I can confirm that she was at the docks meeting with Hal around the time that Stuart was killed, then it might be enough evidence to arrest her. I'm going to bring her in for questioning, as soon as I can find her. Until then, I've ordered the harbor closed and I have a team doing another thorough search of the area for evidence. At this point it might be too late, but I have nothing."

"I'm sure there will be something on the phone that you can use." Suzie smiled.

"I hope so." He frowned. "I keep expecting to come across that one piece of evidence that will break the case, and instead I run into dead ends. The only person who has been cooperative with me is Michael, and that's because he has an alibi." He shook his head and turned back towards his car. "I know the truth is there, I just can't get to it."

"You will, Jason." She smiled as she met his eyes. "I know you will."

"Thanks, Suzie." He glanced at his watch. "I

171

haven't been able to catch up with Lydia, yet. So, I still don't have an alibi for her. I planned to pick her up after the memorial, but she disappeared. I can't figure out where she's staying. Do you know?"

"I'm sorry. Wes might know —" Suzie started.

"No, he doesn't." Mary stepped up quickly. "He doesn't know where she's staying." She locked eyes with Suzie.

"Okay then." Jason nodded as he glanced at Mary. "Are you doing okay?"

"Yes, I'm fine, thanks. Good luck, Jason." Mary glanced over at Suzie again.

"Yes, thanks for coming here so quickly, Jason." Suzie smiled at him. "I'm sure you'll find her, and Hal, soon enough."

"Be safe, ladies." He tipped his hat to them, then headed back to his car.

"What was that about?" Suzie turned to face Mary, her eyes sharp as they locked to her friend's. "What are you hiding?"

"I know where she is." Mary swallowed thickly as she avoided Suzie's eyes.

"What?" Suzie leaned close to her friend as her heartbeat quickened. "You know where she is, and you didn't tell Jason?"

"I know, I know. I'm sorry." Mary released a

long, slow breath. "I saw Wes coming out of her motel room. I thought I should keep it a secret, since he was. He told me that it was important that he didn't reveal too much about his investigation. I figured if he thought Jason needed to know where she was, he would tell him." She squeezed her eyes shut. "But I guess the truth is that he's trying to protect her, and if he's willing to risk his job and Jason's trust, then she must be terribly important to him."

"It may not be that at all. If Wes truly believes that she's innocent that may be why he's protecting her. He might be trying to hide her. I agree, he would never stop Jason from finding Stuart's murderer." She hesitated, then looked up at her friend. "And maybe we need to find out for ourselves before we tell Jason."

"What? Really?" Mary gazed at her as her mouth grew dry. "You want to keep the information from Jason?"

"Not for long. I just want the chance to speak to her about all of this. I mean, if we tell Jason where she is, and he finds out that Wes has been hiding her, Wes could be in some trouble. Not only will Jason be upset, but he could lose his job. Trust me, if he's hurt you, then I want to tear him to pieces, but what if we're wrong about all of this?"

"You're right." Mary nodded slowly as her mind began to churn with the possibilities of the consequences that Wes would face. "I owe it to him to at least hear her side of the story before we throw them both to the wolves." She glanced at her watch. "If we leave now, we can be there in less than twenty minutes. If she's still there, we might have a chance to talk with her."

"Let's go." Suzie started off towards the parking lot.

CHAPTER 15

hen Suzie and Mary arrived at the motel, Mary took the lead. She knocked on the door, then waited. As the seconds passed by, Suzie tipped her head towards the door, and nodded.

Mary knocked harder on the door. After a few moments, the door cracked open.

"Who's out there?" Lydia asked.

"It's Mary. We met before, remember? I'm Wes' girlfriend." Mary tried to meet her eyes through the thin crack in the door. "We're just here to talk with you."

"Who is we?" Her voice sharpened and the door almost shut.

"My friend Suzie is here with me. We just want

to help, if we can. Will you let us in, please?" She leaned a little closer to the door and pressed one hand against it. "Wes and I know each other very well. He trusts me, you can trust me, too."

Mary held her breath as the door pushed closed. She wanted to convince Lydia to let her speak to her, because otherwise she knew that the next step would be to call Jason and let him know where she was. She could only imagine the stand-off that would ensue, with Lydia barricaded behind an old wooden door. Flakes of paint covered the sidewalk she stood on. Had someone else been there, pounding?

"She's not going to let us in." Suzie sighed as she took a step back from the door. She reached into her purse for her phone to call Jason. Before she could pull it out, the door swung open.

"If Wes trusts you, then I'll trust you. I just hope that I don't regret it." Lydia looked nervously between the two of them. Her eyebrows were knitted together, and her lips drawn tight. "Come in quick, I don't want anyone to see me." She gestured for the two to step into the room.

As Mary crossed the threshold into the room, Suzie followed close behind her.

Mary had two children of her own, she couldn't

imagine causing them harm, let alone ever taking their lives. Could Lydia have done something so terrible? Mary couldn't believe it.

"Why are you here?" Lydia began to pace back and forth through the small space. "I know it's for a reason, and it's not to comfort me."

"You're right, it's not." Suzie paused just inside the door. "It's because we want to know what happened to your son, Stuart."

"Oh, do you?" She collapsed onto the couch and closed her eyes. "That's funny, because I'd like to know exactly that."

"Don't play games with me." Suzie crossed her arms as she stared down at the woman. "I know that you were meeting with Hal at about the same time that your son was killed, in the very same place. Are you saying that you had nothing to do with his murder?"

"Suzie." Mary's eyes widened as she wondered if her friend had gone too far.

"I absolutely am saying that I had nothing to do with his murder, because I didn't!" Lydia jumped to her feet and stood right in front of Suzie. "I wasn't the best mother, everyone knows that, but I would never kill my own son. Whoever you got your information from, they're wrong!"

"If you claim you're innocent then tell us where you were when Stuart was killed." Mary stepped forward some as her heart pounded. What if there was another reason why Lydia hadn't come forward with her alibi? What if she was more devious than she had first thought?

"Oh, I'll tell you all right." Lydia crossed her arms and smirked in Mary's direction. "I was right here, with Wes, all night. I'm sure your boyfriend will be more than happy to testify to that."

"You're lying." Mary took a step back as the breath left her body.

"No, I'm not lying, sweetie. Ask Wes about it. He's nothing if he's not honest. He knows I had nothing to do with my son's death, that's why he's been keeping me away from the police. He has his own motive." Lydia rolled her eyes. "That's all I've ever been to men, someone for them to use to get what they want. Wes is no different."

"He's very different," Suzie snapped as she stepped between Mary and Lydia. "You need to start telling the truth. Why did your son call you shortly before he died? What did you two talk about?"

"We didn't talk. He yelled, and I listened. He told me how terrible of a mother I was, and demanded to know why I had been placing bets on his race, and how much money I had lost." Lydia frowned as she stared down at the floor. "I wanted to tell him the truth, about why I was meeting with Hal. I knew that Wes would be upset if I did. So I didn't. I lied to my son, I let him think that I tried to make money from the race, that I bet on the race, something he'd asked me to stop doing. It was our last conversation, and he was furious with me. He said he was going to handle things himself." She wiped a tear from her cheek and took a deep breath. "So, there you have it. My son died thinking I was a terrible person. And he wasn't wrong, I suppose, but I sure wish that I'd had the chance to set the record straight about why I was making the bets."

"Someone met with Hal that night." Mary's voice softened as she realized just how devastating it would be if she lost one of her children. "Can you think of who it might have been?"

"How should I know?" Lydia wiped at her eyes again. "The only other person I know that met with Hal was Alana. She asked me where to find him, actually." She laughed, the sound sharp and bitter. "She was friendly enough to ask me that, but nothing more. After Stuart died, I tried to talk to her about what happened, and she just ignored my calls.

At the memorial, I went up to her, to thank her for helping organize it, and she completely ignored me and walked away. That's why I left. I just couldn't handle it." She sunk down onto the couch again. "Stuart was an amazing athlete. He really was."

"Yes, he was." Mary reached down and took her hand. "Lydia, I'm very sorry for your loss."

"Thank you." Lydia looked up at Mary, her eyes wide. "You're the only person, other than Wes, that has actually been kind to me, Mary. I wasn't lying when I said Wes was here all night. But nothing happened between us. He was here to keep me safe." Her shoulders slumped. "He's a good man you have there, Mary, a very good man."

"Thanks, Lydia." Mary stared into the woman's eyes a moment longer, then followed Suzie to the door. As soon as they were outside, they turned to each other.

"Alana." Suzie narrowed her eyes. "She had no reason to be meeting with Hal, but she went out of her way to find out where he was, from Lydia? Something seems wrong about that."

"Very wrong." Mary nodded. "And she's on her way out of town. I know where the house is that she rented. If we hurry, we might be able to catch her."

~

*O*n the drive to the house, Suzie did her best to concentrate on the road. But her thoughts shifted back to the conversation at the motel. What could Alana have to do with Hal? Was it really possible that she had something to do with Stuart's death?

"I don't know about this." Suzie sighed as she turned down the road that led to the house. "Do we really think she would kill Stuart, and then help organize his memorial?"

"I do." Mary narrowed her eyes as she stared through the windshield. "Or at the very least, she knows who did it. She was on the docks with Hal, I really think she was. Which means she lied about being at the house around the time Stuart was being killed. Which means she told other lies to support her story. If she can lie about that, then maybe she is capable of a lot more."

"Maybe." Suzie frowned.

"Suzie, turn the car around!" Mary pointed to a car that drove towards them. "That's Alana!"

As the car passed them, Suzie caught sight of Alana's face.

"You're right, it is." Suzie drove a little farther, then turned the car around.

"She's headed to the airport. We have to stop her before she gets there." Mary leaned forward as Suzie stepped on the gas. "What are we going to do?"

"I'm not sure. Maybe if I can get in front of her we could do something to slow her down." Suzie sped up, and passed Alana's rental car. Once she was in front of her, she began to slow down. Alana slowed down as well. Ahead of them, a traffic light turned red. Suzie knew it was her only opportunity. Alana would have to stop right behind them, and if she did, then they could find a way to get her out of her car. But then what?

Suzie applied the brakes as she approached the red light.

"Mary, we need to figure out how to get her out of the car."

"I know what to do." Mary opened her door as the car rolled to a stop. She jumped out and ran to the driver's side of Alana's car. She knew the light would change soon, and she had to act fast. As she pounded on the woman's window, Alana stared out at her, shocked.

"What is it, Mary?" She asked as she rolled down the window.

"Alana, I need your help, please, Suzie has lost her mind. She's convinced that Michael is actually the killer and insists she has evidence to prove it. I keep telling her she's crazy, she should go to the police. But she won't listen to me. I've tried calling Jason, but he doesn't answer. I'm afraid if I don't do something to stop her she's going to confront Michael!" She looked desperately back towards the car, then turned to Alana. "Please, I know that you're busy, but when I saw you behind us, I thought you might help."

"I'm not sure how I can help, and besides I have a flight to catch. Just call the police. Tell them she's lost it." Alana shook her head. "The light is green, you'd better get back in your car."

"I can't call the police, what if she's right?" Mary gasped as she clung to the door of the car. "Alana, what if Michael really did kill Stuart and Suzie has something to prove that? If I turn her into the police we may never know for sure what happened to Stuart. Everyone will still be a suspect. She could really have the evidence that solves the crime."

"Do you really think so?" Alana's expression

shifted from annoyed to curious. "What kind of evidence is it?"

"I don't know, she won't tell me. She says she has to drive me to it, she can't explain it. But I'm afraid if she goes to Michael, she's just going to put herself in danger." Mary shuddered. "Suzie can be so determined about things."

"All right, I'll follow you. Just lead the way. If there is something to be found, we should find it. If not, maybe I can calm her down about it." Alana cringed as several cars honked their horns behind them. "Hurry up or someone else will call the police."

"You're right, I'm going." Mary rushed back to the car. She hoped that her plan would work, but she had no idea if Alana would really take the bait.

CHAPTER 16

When Mary climbed back into the car, Suzie looked over at her with wide eyes.

"What did you do?"

"She's following us." Mary buckled her seat belt. "You'd better go, the light is green."

"What?" Suzie looked across the car at her as she pressed on the gas. "What do you mean? What did you tell her?"

"I told her that you knew about evidence that would prove Michael was the killer, so she said she is going to follow us." Mary raised an eyebrow. "Interesting right? If she was the killer, then she would know that Michael wasn't the killer. So why did she agree to follow us?"

"We know that someone tried to frame Michael. Or at least we suspect that someone did. So, let's say that she is the one who framed him. No one knew about his secret binge eating habits, she probably assumed that he was sound asleep at *Dune House* while she killed Stuart. Therefore, he would be the perfect person to take the fall." Suzie flicked on the turn signal and turned off the main highway. As she glanced in the rearview mirror, she saw Alana do the same thing. "But him having a solid alibi threw a wrench into her plans. Maybe she thinks whatever evidence we have, will be enough to put him back in the hot seat, and take the focus off everyone else. If she is the killer, she won't feel safe until someone is arrested for Stuart's murder."

"Yes! That makes sense, Suzie. It could be possible." She looked over her shoulder, then back at Suzie. "Listen, I told her that you had gone a little crazy. So, you may have to put on a bit of a show when we get to where we're going."

"And where exactly is that?" Suzie winced. "I'm just driving for the sake of driving right now. We don't have any evidence that Michael is the killer. What do you think is going to happen when we have nothing to show her?"

"Maybe we can pretend that we have evidence

and use it as a way to trap her, to get her to confess that she knows that Michael is innocent because she is the one who killed Stuart." Mary frowned. "Turn down this street, let's head for the docks. That should get her nervous if she is the killer."

"Okay, good idea. No one will be there though, Jason ordered the harbor clear of people so he could search for additional evidence." Suzie glanced at the darkening sky. "I'm sure they are done with their search for the day."

"That's all right, that will give us the chance to fabricate some kind of evidence and get a confession from her, hopefully." Mary searched her mind for a plan.

"Better think of something fast, because we're almost there." Suzie slowed down, hoping to draw out the process. Then she veered the car a little to the left, and then to the right, to give the impression that she really was behaving erratically.

"We'll tell her that we found some blood spatter from the gunshot. We found it on Michael's shirt. We'll see how she reacts. If she's not the killer she might believe us. If she is the killer, she might be too tempted to see it and try to use it to frame Michael. At least we might find out something from her reaction. Do you think it will work?" Mary's voice trembled.

"It will have to, because we're here." Suzie pulled into a parking space, and turned off the engine. She wondered if they would be able to pull off the plan.

As Suzie stepped onto the wooden planks of the dock, she noticed that it was completely deserted. There were no lights on any of the boats. No voices could be heard over the subtle lapping of the water. Was it like this when Stuart died?

The sharp sound of Alana's car door made her jump. She turned as the woman stepped up onto the dock as well. Her expression was colder than she expected, and eerily calm.

"Well ladies, I guess we have some things to settle." Alana pulled a gun from her purse and aimed it directly at Suzie. "We're alone out here you know? I thought, as I followed you, they couldn't be this stupid, could they? But here we are."

"Alana, what are you doing?" Mary gasped and stepped closer to Suzie. "You have no reason to do this!"

"No reason?" Alana raised an eyebrow. "Did you really think that I wouldn't see through the little plan that you concocted? I'm not an idiot. I could have just gone to the airport, but I knew you two wouldn't stop. I can't move on with my life with your suspicion hanging over my head. Eventually you would find something, some clue that would be tied directly to what I did, and then I would be back in the same position I am now. I can't live like that. Can anyone really?"

"So, you did do it?" Suzie flinched as she took a step back. She didn't like the barrel of the gun pointed at her. A quick glance up and down the docks proved that Alana was right. No one was there, and most people in town were still at the memorial. It wasn't likely that anyone would even hear a gunshot. In the distance, she thought she could hear Pilot barking. "You killed Stuart?"

"I did what had to be done. I had no choice in the matter." Alana huffed as she adjusted her aim to Suzie's chest. "In the first place I didn't want Stuart at the race. He had too many demands, and therefore simply cost too much. But his agent insisted, and I couldn't turn him down. I knew I wouldn't have the money to cover the race, so I decided to rig the race. I placed a heavy bet on Michael's team winning, then I had Michael take Simon out. I knew he would never admit to crashing into Simon deliberately, because of the consequences to him and his career. Without Simon in the race, I knew that they wouldn't be able to replace him at such short notice, and even if they could Stuart would probably quit. He was the only real competition against Michael's team. Everything would have been just fine." She released the safety on the gun.

"Please don't, Alana. You're not this person, you're not a murderer!" Mary grimaced as she watched the woman continue to take aim at her best friend.

"But I am. I am because I had to be. Hal heard the accusations that Michael did it on purpose, and that he would likely be disqualified. He wanted money. He demanded it. I didn't have it." Alana narrowed her eyes. "I wanted to meet with him to calm him down, tell him that it would be okay. Michael wouldn't be disqualified. The race would happen and then he would get the money. I met with him on the docks, and Stuart just happened to show up at the right time to witness it all. He threatened to tell everyone, it would have ruined me, I would have ended up in prison for orchestrating the attack on Simon. I knew that I had no choice. So, I killed him. Then I knew I had to get rid of the body. I had stolen a couple of sheets and a towel from *Dune House* when I walked through it earlier in the day. The house we are staying at doesn't provide linen, and I forgot to bring some with me. Money isn't exactly abundant at the moment, so I didn't want to waste it. Turns out it was lucky I forgot to bring them. I remembered that Michael was staying at *Dune House*, and I decided I would pin the murder on him. So, I took the sheet from my car, and wrapped Stuart's body in it, attached the weight, then rolled it into the water. I guess my knot tying abilities are not great." She frowned. "I thought I'd have some time before the body was found. The race would go on, I would get the money, and I would be able to pay everything off. But then Stuart's body popped up, and all of that changed."

"And Michael's alibi left you with no one to blame the murder on." Suzie crossed her arms, though her eyes never left Alana's finger on the trigger.

"And you never had any evidence to implicate Michael. I knew that. If there was anything to find, I would have found it. That's why I followed you here. Because I knew you two suspected me, and I had to put an end to it. As soon as I am rid of you I can pin the murder on Charles, which is what I should have done in the first place. He has insomnia and I found out he was walking along the docks that night. He hasn't told the police, because he knows he will look guilty." Alana gestured to Suzie with the gun. "Move closer to the water. I've learned from my mistakes. This time they won't find your body for months."

"Alana, there are other ways we can work this out." Mary fought against the urge to grab Suzie's hand. She knew that any sudden move might convince Alana to pull the trigger. Panic welled up deep within her as she realized that no one knew where they were.

"Move I said, or I'll start with your friend!" Alana swung the gun towards Mary.

"No don't!" Suzie gasped and moved back to the edge of the dock. Her heels stuck out just over the edge.

"Perfect." Alana nodded. She kept the gun trained on Suzie as she walked over to a pile of cement blocks. "These should do just fine."

"Alana, stop this, now!" Suzie started to take a step towards her.

"Not another step!" She turned her attention directly on to Suzie again.

The barrel of the gun pointed at her face silenced Suzie. Her heart skipped a beat. Yes, she'd been in dangerous situations before, but nothing like this. She held her breath as she prepared for the bullet to strike her.

"Alana, please." Mary's gentle voice reached out to the woman. "Be reasonable. Suzie has done nothing to you. Neither have I. We're not unreasonable people. We can work out some kind of agreement. We can even steer the authorities in a new direction." Mary nodded as she took a small step closer to Alana.

"Enough!" Alana scowled in her direction. "Neither of you are getting out of here alive, I'm just waiting for the right moment." She glanced up at the sky, then back over at Suzie and Mary. "I don't care if two nobodies from a nobody town end up dead. It's nothing compared to the fantastic life I will lead. You will never matter as much as I do."

"Fine, maybe that is the case, but I know something that you don't." Suzie forced each word between trembling lips as the gun remained trained on her. "Something that does matter."

"What?" Alana narrowed her eyes as she looked at Suzie with interest. "This is just some kind of trick, isn't it? You're buying time. But no worries, in only a few minutes, all of this will be over."

"It's not a trick, it's a warning." Suzie tried to

inch forward on the dock, but it was impossible to move her feet while keeping her balance.

"Fine, what is it?" Alana took a step towards her. The gun hovered only inches away from Suzie's nose.

CHAPTER 17

"We're not alone." Suzie braced herself as she sensed how close to the edge her feet were. The sight of the gun so close to her face made her stomach twist with fear. "My boyfriend Paul is on his boat, and all it takes is one scream from me to alert him that there is a problem. He'll have the police here in seconds."

"Liar." Alana laughed and lowered the gun just a few inches. "I saw him at the memorial, he was still there when I left." She tipped her head to the side as she smiled. "Did you forget to tell him that you had this little operation planned?"

"Yes, he did stay after I left the memorial, but I called him after. I told him I'd be headed to the docks, and asked him to hang out on his boat just in case I needed him." She glanced in the direction of Paul's boat. "All I have to do is make a sound."

"Don't!" Alana shoved the gun towards her as she snapped out the word. "You open your mouth and I will kill you both before Paul can even pick up his phone. Then, I'll take care of him, too. You have no idea what I am willing to do to save my business, my career."

"It's just money!" Mary cried out, desperation took her breath away. "Please Alana! Think clearly!"

"Oh, I'm thinking clearly all right. It isn't just money to me." She waved the gun briefly at Mary, then pointed it at Suzie again. "It's everything I've worked so hard for. It's my business, my life. I will never be able to recover my reputation. I don't have a family. This is it for me. This has been my whole life, and now, you think you can just take that from me?" She glared between the two women. "Stuart was a lost cause, and everyone knows that. His mother did a number on him, so sad, but it doesn't change the fact that he was a worthless waste of space, and I did the world a favor by getting rid of him. You two, you've had good lives I'm sure, now they're over. I'm sorry, but that's just how it has to be."

"It doesn't have to be that way." Suzie blinked back tears. She knew that Paul was nowhere near his boat. He was at *Dune House* waiting for her. He probably didn't even miss her, yet. There was no one to come to their rescue. "Just slow down, let's talk about this. We can figure out a solution that will work for all of us."

"There is only one solution!" Alana aimed the gun straight at Suzie's forehead.

"Drop it now!" Wes' commanding voice made Suzie's body jerk with surprise.

Mary grabbed Suzie's hand as she teetered at the edge of the water and pulled her onto the dock.

"You!" Alana spun around with her weapon still in her hand. As she aimed it at Wes, it was clear that she intended to pull the trigger.

"No!" Mary lunged for Alana, with her arms spread wide. When she collided with the woman's mid-section, she realized that they were both headed for the water.

"Mary!" Suzie's scream was the last thing that Mary heard before the splash of the water all around her. She went under with Alana still tangled in her arms. As she pushed away from the woman, Alana swam towards the surface. Mary struggled her way back up as well, just in time to see Wes drag Alana from the water.

"Mary, take my hand." Suzie thrust her hand out to her.

"Thank you, Suzie." Mary drew in a deep breath and between Suzie's tugging and her determination she managed to get back up on the dock. "Wes, are you okay?" She grimaced as she got to her feet.

"I'm fine." He snapped handcuffs on Alana's wrists. "Thanks to you." He met her eyes and smiled.

"How did you find us?" Mary stared at him with wide eyes.

"I wanted to speak to you after the memorial, but you left before I had the chance. Since I found out Hal might be involved in this I helped Jason and he managed to get him into custody. Then I arranged it so Jason could speak to Lydia, she mentioned seeing the two of you. I knew then I had to find you both. So, I put a be-on-the-lookout order for your car, and Suzie's."

Wes glanced over his shoulder at the sound of sirens. With one hand clenched on Alana's arm, he gave her a slight tug backwards.

"There's your ride."

"Let me go!" Alana grunted and strained against the handcuffs. "You will never prove anything."

"It's too late for that, Alana." Suzie pulled off her jacket and draped it around Mary's shoulders. "Mary and I both heard your confession, you're going to prison. It's over."

A police car pulled into the parking lot. As the tires squealed, and the siren blared, Suzie finally felt relief. It really was over.

Wes turned Alana over to the officer who jogged up to them, then he turned to face Mary.

"One of the officers in Parish spotted Suzie's car and was able to tail her for some time, but he got called away to an emergency. I knew you were headed in this direction, so I decided to check at *Dune House*, and here. I saw Suzie's car in the parking lot." He grabbed Mary by her shoulders and pulled her close to him. "Promise me, you will never, ever, do that again."

"Do what?" Mary looked into his eyes.

"Put yourself in danger to protect me." Wes stroked the curve of her cheek.

"I'm sorry, Wes, I can't promise you that." Mary gazed into his eyes. "I will always do absolutely everything in my power to keep you safe."

"Oh Mary." Wes sighed and kissed her forehead. "How did I ever get so lucky?"

"Luckier than you were in high school?" She raised an eyebrow.

"There was, and is, nothing between Lydia and me." He smiled some as he pulled her close again. "I know that Lydia has already told you part of the story. Now that the investigation is over, I can tell you everything. I asked Lydia for her help to investigate Hal. He'd been accepting illegal bets for a long time, and would hire thugs to hunt down people who didn't pay. I knew that she knew him quite well from when she lived in Parish. I also knew that she'd be in town for Stuart's race. So, I asked her to work with me to get evidence against Hal. She agreed." He tucked a few strands of her hair behind her ear. "It was only ever business. I do care for her as a friend, as someone who went through rougher times than anyone should have, but that is all. I hope you can trust me."

"I do." Mary leaned in for a quick kiss. "I absolutely do, Wes."

"Suzie! Mary! Are you okay?" Jason ran towards them from the parking lot of the docks. "I've just been caught up on what happened."

"We're okay." Suzie took a deep breath. "But

there's one more arrest you need to make. Michael really did crash into and injure Simon on purpose. He may not have had anything to do with Stuart's death, but he shouldn't get away with what he did to Simon."

"I'll get someone to pick him up right away." Jason nodded, then stepped away with his radio in his hand.

As Suzie turned back to look over the water, a ripple of fear carried through her. She'd almost met the same end as Stuart, were it not for Wes, she might have. All she wanted, was one thing.

"Suzie." Paul's voice drifted over her shoulder. "Suzie, I've been looking for you everywhere."

"Paul." Suzie turned to face him with a warm smile. Her wish had been answered. As she wrapped her arms around him, she held on as tight as she could. Yes, she had a very good life, and she was relieved that it hadn't come to an abrupt end. Alana would pay for her crime, Stuart would be laid to rest, and she would try to enjoy every moment.

The End

ALSO BY CINDY BELL

WAGGING TAIL COZY MYSTERIES

Murder at Pooch Park

DUNE HOUSE COZY MYSTERIES

Seaside Secrets

Boats and Bad Guys

Treasured History

Hidden Hideaways

Dodgy Dealings

Suspects and Surprises

Ruffled Feathers

A Fishy Discovery

Danger in the Depths

Celebrities and Chaos

Pups, Pilots and Peril

Tides, Trails and Trouble

Racing and Robberies

SAGE GARDENS COZY MYSTERIES

Birthdays Can Be Deadly

Money Can Be Deadly

Trust Can Be Deadly

Ties Can Be Deadly

Rocks Can Be Deadly

Jewelry Can Be Deadly

Numbers Can Be Deadly

Memories Can Be Deadly

Paintings Can Be Deadly

Snow Can Be Deadly

Tea Can Be Deadly

CHOCOLATE CENTERED COZY MYSTERIES

The Sweet Smell of Murder

A Deadly Delicious Delivery

A Bitter Sweet Murder

A Treacherous Tasty Trail

Pastry and Peril

Trouble and Treats

Fudge Films and Felonies

Custom-Made Murder

Skydiving, Soufflés and Sabotage

Christmas Chocolates and Crimes

Hot Chocolate and Homicide

Chocolate Caramels and Conmen

Picnics, Pies and Lies

DONUT TRUCK COZY MYSTERIES

Deadly Deals and Donuts

Fatal Festive Donuts

Bunny Donuts and a Body

BEKKI THE BEAUTICIAN COZY MYSTERIES

Hairspray and Homicide

A Dyed Blonde and a Dead Body

Mascara and Murder

Pageant and Poison

Conditioner and a Corpse

Mistletoe, Makeup and Murder

Hairpin, Hair Dryer and Homicide

Blush, a Bride and a Body

Shampoo and a Stiff

Cosmetics, a Cruise and a Killer

Lipstick, a Long Iron and Lifeless

Camping, Concealer and Criminals

Treated and Dyed

A Wrinkle-Free Murder

A MACARON PATISSERIE COZY MYSTERY SERIES

Sifting for Suspects

Recipes and Revenge

Mansions, Macarons and Murder

NUTS ABOUT NUTS COZY MYSTERIES

A Tough Case to Crack

A Seed of Doubt

Roasted Penuts and Peril

HEAVENLY HIGHLAND INN COZY MYSTERIES

Murdering the Roses

Dead in the Daisies

Killing the Carnations

Drowning the Daffodils

Suffocating the Sunflowers

Books, Bullets and Blooms

A Deadly Serious Gardening Contest

A Bridal Bouquet and a Body

Digging for Dirt

WENDY THE WEDDING PLANNER COZY MYSTERIES

Matrimony, Money and Murder

Chefs, Ceremonies and Crimes

Knives and Nuptials

Mice, Marriage and Murder

ABOUT THE AUTHOR

Cindy Bell is a USA Today and Wall Street Journal Bestselling Author. She is the author of the cozy mystery series Wagging Tail, Donut Truck, Dune House, Sage Gardens, Chocolate Centered, Macaron Patisserie, Nuts about Nuts, Bekki the Beautician, Heavenly Highland Inn and Wendy the Wedding Planner.

Cindy has always loved reading, but it is only recently that she has discovered her passion for writing romantic cozy mysteries. She loves walking along the beach thinking of the next adventure her characters can embark on.

You can sign up for her newsletter so you are notified of her latest releases at http://www.cindybellbooks.com.

Made in the USA
Columbia, SC
18 June 2020